Under the Peach Tree

Under the Peach Tree

Charlay Marie

www.urbanchristianonline.com

Urban Books, LLC
97 N18th Street
Wyandanch, NY 11798

Under the Peach Tree Copyright © 2014 Charlay Marie

All rights reserved. No part of this book may be reproduced in any form or by any means without prior consent of the Publisher, excepting brief quotes used in reviews.

ISBN 13: 978-1-60162-779-7
ISBN 10: 1-60162-779-3

First Trade Paperback Printing June 2014
Printed in the United States of America

10 9 8 7 6 5 4 3 2 1

This is a work of fiction. Any references or similarities to actual events, real people, living or dead, or to real locales are intended to give the novel a sense of reality. Any similarity in other names, characters, places, and incidents is entirely coincidental.

Distributed by Kensington Corp.
Submit Wholesale Orders to:
Kensington Publishing Corp.
C/O Penguin Group (USA) Inc.
Attention: Order Processing
405 Murray Hill Parkway
East Rutherford, NJ 07073-2316
Phone: 1-800-526-0275
Fax: 1-800-227-9604

Acknowledgments

I give all of my thanks and the glory to God. This is the first of many great works God has given me that He had set out from the beginning for me to do. And who am I but just a sinner who God has looked down on and found favor? I thank you, Jesus! I thank you for bringing wonderful people into my life who have helped bring this book to life.

Like my best friend, Star. She has helped me with ideas and story plotting whenever I got stuck in the story. She's listened enthusiastically to every brainstorming moment and epiphany, especially the ones that came while she was watching TV or doing something important. She's kept me motivated by being my number one fan, for believing in my story when I began to second-guess. She promotes me and my book everywhere we go, like she is my spokesperson or personal cheerleader! LOL. If it weren't for God giving me such a supportive best friend, this book may have not been written.

I would also like to thank God for my mom and dad . . . and their genes. They had three talented, smart daughters who are inclined to write. If it had not been for my sisters Nikki's and Tisha's poems and stories, I would have not been inspired to be just like them and write. They were the girls who graduated top of their class, with published poems and beautiful writing skills. I hope that I can now encourage the both of them to continue writing, as they have done with me.

Acknowledgments

God has placed other people in my life who have helped me with this book deal. I'd like to give thanks to Renea Collins, author of *From the Extreme* and *I Repent,* who was kind enough to refer me to her editor, Joylynn M. Ross, so that I could pitch my book for a possible book deal. Joylynn, I thank you for believing in my book and taking it on as my editor, when I had been turned down by two other publishing companies. I want to thank Urban Books for publishing my first novel.

Many blessings to the people who I haven't mentioned who have helped me with this book in some way. I want to thank all of my supporters who are reading this book. I ask that Jesus allows this book to touch hearts all around the world, to deliver and minister to those in need, to break chains and generational curses, to heal past hurt or regret, and to allow forgiveness to manifest in the hearts of those reading. Thank you, Jesus! All glory to God!

Prologue

I felt a presence behind me, or maybe I felt the wind blowing past. However, I turned around and saw Momma. She was much older than I remembered, with wrinkles swallowing her fragile face. It had only been ten years and yet her back was hunched over from working so hard. Instinct told me to run to her, take her in my arms, and hold her. It'd been years since I saw her face. However, I couldn't bring myself to hug a woman who never seemed to love me.

I smeared tears into my skin as I tried to wipe them away. *Faith*. I needed my sister. "Momma, where's Faith?"

The tree casted an eerie shadow over Momma's face as she slowly shook her head. I knew what she'd say even before the words slurred out of her mouth: "Faith is gone. She went to be with the Lord."

The memory of an incident becomes faded with time. It's the pain that lingers, a venomous snake waiting for an opportunity to strike. I was sure that if my soul were visible, it'd have been masked with battle wounds. But I wore those scars proudly. They were reminders that I'd made it, that I was still making it. The devil was not successful in his pursuit to destroy me.

However, there was a time in my life where I would have said otherwise.

Chapter 1

Even at the age of nine, I understood there was a favorable difference between me and my twin, Faith. Children shouldn't have to experience favoritism from their parents, but I did. Momma would always put Faith in the prettiest of dresses, brush her fine hair into a silky bun with a little ribbon, and get her toenails painted. Faith got to go to church with Grandma on Sundays while I stayed at home, nappy-headed and dirty from fighting the neighborhood boys. I didn't get the chance to know who Jesus was, but Faith did.

Maybe that's why Momma named her Faith and me Hope, because faith is greater than hope. Everyone has hope, but it's their faith that sees them through. Momma must've known early on that the lighter twin, who came first out of her womanhood, would be the good twin.

I remember the day when I realized the difference between the two of us. Faith was twirling in the living room, admiring her pretty pink dress as Momma combed through my naps. I watched her twirl, wishing I had a dress that pretty, wishing Momma would put my hair in that bun.

I looked at her black shiny dress shoes scuffing the wood floor. Faith's socks were white and pink with pretty ruffles at the top. She looked like a poster child from an Easter catalog. Momma always put her hair in a bun because it was too thick and curly to manage. My hair was too short and nappy for a bun, so all Momma would do was put it into a few pigtails and snap barrettes at the ends. My hair used to stick up each and every way; I remember the kids making fun of me for it. But Momma never cared about me; she'd still send me outside looking like a boy.

"Hope, watch how my dress puffs up when I twirl!" Faith said, demonstrating her perfect spin again. It reminded me of the ballerinas I watched on TV. I tried to jump up and twirl with her, but Momma snatched my hair and yanked my head back.

"Sit down, Hope!" she warned, her voice low and steady. It was the voice she used whenever a spanking was around the corner. The memory of my most recent butt whoopin' made my bottom sting. "I'm 'bout tired of you."

Faith stopped twirling and took a seat on the couch. She was waiting for Grandma to come pick her up for church. Grandma usually came on time unless she was trying to look extra spiffy for the church folk. I once heard that everybody at the church tried to out-dress each other. Grandma used to think she was so fly but I always thought she looked casket ready. I once told her that and got smacked upside my head.

"Momma," I said carefully, making sure my head didn't move an inch. I didn't want to get smacked with the brush. "Can I go to church with Faith today?"

"You don't got a dress."

"I can wear one of Faith's dresses. She got a lot," I said enthusiastically.

"You too chunky for her dresses. If you try to squeeze into it, them church men's gonna look at you the wrong way."

I didn't understand what she meant. Yes, I was chunkier than Faith. Momma said I was already starting to develop at nine, but I fit in those dresses fine whenever Faith would let me play dress-up in her room.

"Can you buy me a pretty dress, then?"

Momma smirked. "So you can go to church and act a fool? No. Your grandma will only take one of you, the good twin. She said so herself."

Her words stung but I knew she was right. Grandma didn't seem to like me as much as Faith. I folded my arms at the same time Faith did, and her face also fell to match my own, hurt.

Later that day, after Grandma picked up Faith for church, I went outside in a shirt and dirty jeans to play. Momma knew I was rough outside and didn't dare dress me in anything pretty. I fought too much. I had to. The neighborhood boys always picked on me. Faith said it was because they liked me, but I didn't believe that. They always said I was ugly.

I was sitting near my favorite peach tree, listening to the church choir sing. It was the typical white country church with white pillars, a big bell that sat on the roof, a white picket fence, and a cemetery in the backyard. I always wanted to see what was inside, but Momma would never let me go, and since I couldn't go, I just enjoyed it from the outside. I had a favorite song they would sing almost every Sunday. The church sat half a mile down the street, but in the country, loud noises traveled and fast.

"'Nobody knows de trouble I've seen . . . nobody knows de trouble but Jesus!'" I didn't know who Jesus was, but they always sang about him. "'Nobody knows de trouble I've seen, Glory Hallelujah!'"

"Shut yo' butt up, singing like you at church!"

I didn't have to turn around and look to know who stood behind me. It was Jordan and his four friends. I heard them snickering in the background. I finally turned around and met trouble with my head high.

"Well, one day I will sing at church and all you ugly boys gonna feel stupid," I spat. They didn't scare me.

Jordan still had the black eye I gave him a few days ago. Just remembering the butt whoopin' I got by my momma made me shiver, but I'd do it again in a heartbeat. Boys like him deserved to get beat up every day.

"No, you ain't, ugly. I heard my momma talkin' on the phone about how your grandmomma only takes the pretty twin to church to show off in front of them church folk! My momma said you can't go to church no how because the devil can't enter the holy place."

The word "devil" triggered something deep inside, angering me beyond belief. I had been called the devil too many times in my life. I noticed a thick rock lying by the tree. I picked it up and threw it at his head. I smiled as the rock made impact with a loud thud. I sneered as Jordan fell to the ground, holding his head. "Don't nobody call me the devil except my momma!"

At the time, I didn't know that it was wrong even for Momma to say it.

"Here," Faith said, handing me some ice for my cheek. She had changed out of her Sunday dress and set it on my bed. She started playing with her fingers the way she always did whenever she had something on her mind. "I heard Momma tell Grandma that she had to smack the mess out of you because you busted Jordan's head open, so I brought you some ice. What did he do to you, Hope?"

I placed the ice on my cheek, temporarily relieved. Momma had done a lot more than just smack me, but I didn't tell Faith that. "Jordan and his friends came messing with me today, talking about how I can't go to church because I'm the devil." I paused, feeling sadness sweep over me. I heard Momma say it so many times but I didn't think other people would say it too. If everyone thought I was the devil, then it must've been true. "Faith, do you think I'm the devil?"

"No, Hope, you ain't the devil. You an angel," Faith said. She sat down on my bed and began playing with the dress she set on my bed earlier. "The preacher at church always talking about the devil; said he was an angel that fell because he was really bad."

"Well what did he fall off of?"

Faith laughed. "He fell from heaven, which is where God and all the good angels live. It's where you and me gonna go live one day."

I thought about what she said for a moment and then turned to her. "Why would God let me go to heaven if Momma won't even let me go to church?"

"Well, the preacher said that God loves everybody."

"Does that mean Momma don't love me?" I asked.

"No, Momma loves you, just in a different way than she loves me." Faith was so sure of it and reminded me every day. Momma loved me, just differently. Well, even at nine years old I knew loving two kids unequally wasn't right. But there was nothing I could do about it except try to make Momma love me. I sighed, watching Faith set her pink dress in my lap. "Here, I wanna give you my new dress."

I held back my tears, which was something I learned to do whenever I got picked on or whooped, and that was often. Momma whooped me at least two times a day. Sometimes I didn't even know what I did.

"But Momma just got this dress for you," I said.

"I want you to have it. It's too big on me, and I think it will look prettier on you."

I stood up and began undressing as quickly as I could. Faith always knew what to do to make me happy again. It's how it'd always been. I was always down and Faith would come along to pick me back up. Whenever those boys called me ugly, it was Faith who told me I was pretty. When my momma would call me fat, Faith would tell me I was the perfect size. Whenever Momma said I had nappy hair and wished my hair was like Faith's, my sister would tell me that there was no such thing as good or bad hair. Deep down, I always believed everyone else. Faith was just being nice to me. It's what sisters did. They looked out for each other.

After I had the dress on, I turned around to Faith so she could see. She examined me and smiled like I was the most beautiful person in the world.

"It looks so pretty on you!" she said, even though I couldn't zip it all the way up in the back. "You look like a baby doll! Do you wanna play momma and daughter?"

I nodded cheerfully. It was my favorite game because Faith always pretended to be the momma I always wished I had. Faith held me in her arms and kissed my sore cheek. "You're so pretty, baby. Momma's little girl. I love you so much!"

"I love you too, Momma!" I smiled and melted into my twin's arms.

Chapter 2

At twelve years old, I was still defending myself against the neighborhood kids. "Fight! Fight! Fight! Fight!" I heard all the kids screaming around me, but I only saw big, fat Dee Dee cracking her knuckles. She was Jordan's bigger sister and was twice my size. She was baldheaded and tried to wear a ponytail but her hair wouldn't stay in it, so, instead, it stuck out at all places. She was known for bullying all of the younger kids around the way, but I was never scared of her. I was big for my age too, and would beat her up like I did her brother.

A week ago, Jordan asked me to make Faith be his girlfriend, and if I didn't, he'd get his sister to beat me up. Momma told Faith that she could have a boyfriend when she turned sixteen, and she still had four years to go. Momma told me that I couldn't have a boyfriend until I was eighteen. I didn't understand why until Faith explained it was because I already had big boobs at twelve, and that Momma said I already looked sixteen and would probably be the first to have a baby, so no boyfriends until I was grown.

I didn't think it was fair though. Momma always had an excuse for why Faith got to do things that I couldn't and half of the time it never made sense.

"Why you look scared now, Hope? You wasn't scared all those times you fought my little brother," Dee Dee said, breaking my reverie.

I smacked my lips and rolled my eyes sarcastically. "Dee Dee, ain't nobody even scared of you. All you gonna do is try to sit on me with your fat self!" I heard everybody laugh, which added fuel to the fire I was already standing in. Down the road, I could see Faith running toward us. Momma still had her dressed in those pretty dresses. I admired how it danced in the wind as she ran. I still wasn't able to wear dresses, but I guess pants and a T-shirt was the best thing to fight in.

My attention snapped back to Dee Dee as she clenched her fist, ready to punch me. I looked back at Faith, who was just feet away. Her shouts temporarily distracted everyone.

"Hope!" She ran up to me, oblivious to the fight that I was about to be in. She bent down, resting her hands on her knees while trying to catch her breath. "Hope, the street lights are on. Momma's gonna kill you if she finds out you're still outside! Come on!" Faith grabbed my arm and started dragging me away.

"Look, she's running away, scared to get her butt beat!" Dee Dee shouted as we ran down the street. But I didn't care; if Momma knew I was still outside, she'd do far worse to me than Dee Dee ever could.

Faith and I snuck into the house through the back door. The kitchen smelled like fresh rolls and pork chops. My stomach started to growl, I hadn't eaten a thing all day. But that wasn't unusual; we never had food in the house. Or maybe it was because Momma told me I needed to stop eating so much because I was chunky. I used to hate watching Faith eat snacks and candy while I had nothing.

"Come on!" Faith whispered, after peeking around the wall to see if Momma was sitting in the living room. "She looks like she's sleeping."

She grabbed my arm and pulled me down the hallway. Once we were in her room, she flopped down on her bed and relaxed. "If Momma knew you were still outside, she would've blacked your eye!"

I laughed. "But she didn't. She probably fell asleep watching her shows. You know she wanted to see if Bobby was going to leave Christina for Angie."

"I watched it with her." Faith laughed. "And Bobby did leave Christina but only because she's pregnant by Bobby's brother. And why were you outside with all those kids?"

"Big, fat Dee Dee wanted to beat me up because I won't let Jordan be your boyfriend."

Faith's eyes widened. "Jordan wants to be my boyfriend?"

"Yes, and Momma said you can't date until your sixteen. Plus, Jordan is ugly!"

"No, he's not! All of the girls in the seventh and eighth grade like him, too! I heard an eighth grader saying she wanted to do it to him!"

"Ew!" I started to choke, like I was dying.

"And he's sweet to me," Faith said in a dreamlike state.

"Well, he's mean to me, and I don't want you talking to him!"

Faith was quiet for a minute. I watched her fiddle with her fingers in contemplation.

"What is it, Faith?"

"Nothing," she mumbled, keeping her eyes averted.

"No, tell me! You never keep anything from me."

Faith sighed. "I started my period today."

I laughed. "About time! What did Momma say?"

"She was happy, I guess. Said I'm finally becoming a woman."

I frowned. "Momma whooped my butt when she found out when I started. Remember? She said I was doing the nasty with them little boys because eleven-year-old girls don't get periods and it had to be my cherry, whatever that means. And when the doctor told her it was my period, she didn't apologize for beating me."

"I'm sorry about that, Hope," Faith said, as if it was her fault.

"Why do you always apologize for Momma's actions?"

Faith shrugged. "Everybody deserves an apology. When I went to church last Sunday, the preacher said everybody should also forgive those who sin against us."

"What's sin?"

"It's when people do bad things that Jesus tells them not to do. He has a lot of rules that we're supposed to listen to. Like we're not supposed to steal, or lie, or kill, and we have to love God first," she explained.

"How many rules are there?"

"Too many to count."

I nodded and tried to picture the preacher preaching the words that my twin had the privilege of hearing. I learned at an early age to hate church. If God wanted me to go, He'd have me there. But I still sat outside near the church every Sunday and sang all the church songs. Mostly because I loved to sing; partly because I didn't want to feel left out.

Momma didn't go to church either. Whenever I asked her, she would say because it's boring and her momma used to make her go to church as a little girl. She told me I better be thankful that I didn't have to sit there and listen to an old man talk about a God who she never heard nor saw. She said that maybe when she got old and had no choice she would finally set foot back in church.

No church attendance: it's something both me and my momma had in common.

"Faith, do you think that God knows who I am?"

She smiled. "He knows all His children. At least that's what the preacher said."

"So, God and Momma was together?"

Faith laughed. "No! God is Momma's father too!"

"I don't get it," I stated, confused.

"Me either, but I'll ask the preacher next Sunday and tell you."

I lowered my head. "Faith, do you think Momma will start letting me go to church?"

"Ask her."

A week later, I finally worked up enough nerve to ask my mother. She was cooking breakfast Sunday morning, singing an Earth, Wind & Fire song. She was in a very good mood, probably because she no longer had to worry about doing our hair; Faith did both of ours. She didn't have to worry about picking out our clothes or getting us dressed. All she did on Sunday was cook and watch TV.

Being twelve years old also meant that I no longer got whooped. Instead, she'd just smack me upside my head and send me to my room with no dinner. I preferred the beatings. I also felt like my mother never took the time to even see if I was in the wrong whenever she accused me of doing something. She never heard my side of the story. To her, I was guilty with no chance of being proven innocent. I was the bad twin, the fat twin, the nappy-haired twin, the devil twin. Faith was the good twin, the sweet twin, the pretty twin, the polite twin, the angel. Momma said we were like night and day, but Faith and I knew better. We were just alike. We were twins. The thing I loved most about Faith was that she never saw herself as better than me. We were equals, the same on the inside, just different on the outside.

I never understood why Momma treated us differently. I used to lie up at night praying for God to make me a good girl so that Momma would love me more. No matter how hard I tried, she still found something to pick at. Eventually I accepted my fate, but it didn't make it less hurtful.

I used to leave Momma drawings with hearts and kisses all over them to show her how much I loved her, but she always regarded them as trash, and I'd find them lying in the garbage hours later. Faith got to keep her drawings on the refrigerator. Momma said it was because she was good at drawing and her pictures should be shown off, but I didn't believe that.

"Momma, can I start going to church?"

"No, and don't ask again." Her tone of voice was final. I decided to direct the conversation elsewhere.

"Hey, Momma, what are you cooking?"

"I'm cooking some breakfast for Faith before she goes to church."

I frowned. "What about my breakfast?"

"I only have enough to make Faith breakfast. She's the one who gotta go to church. Don't want her around them church folk hungry. There's some crackers in the cabinet, eat them!"

I turned around and saw Faith standing in the doorway, watching. Her expression was impassive, but I know she felt what I felt. Momma had bought Faith a new dress and that's why she didn't have any money to put groceries in the house. Knowing Faith, she'd think it was her fault that I didn't get any breakfast.

I decided not to argue about it, and walked over to the cabinet to get the crackers, but the cabinet was empty.

"Ain't no crackers," I said, turning around to Momma with a frown.

She sighed. "Oh, that's right. I gave them to Jordan's mom so that they could eat them with some chili she made last night."

I sighed and rubbed my growling stomach. I couldn't believe Momma would give her last food to the neighbors but couldn't give me a thing. I didn't understand how a mother could let her child go hungry and not think twice about it. I bet if I died, she wouldn't have even blinked.

***

Grandma no longer picked Faith up for church since she was old enough to walk. Every Sunday, I would walk Faith up to the entrance of the church and then go over to my peach tree and sing the songs. Once we were out of our house, Faith handed me her lunch.

"Here, take it. " She shoved her food in my hands.

"Then what are you gonna eat, Faith?"

"I'm not hungry, okay? If you don't eat, I don't eat."

I smiled. Her generosity was her best trait. "Thanks."

We continued walking down the road in silence. I was admiring the beautiful South Carolina day. The sun was shining brightly and the trees danced in the wind. Days like these were the best. There was something about the sound of nature that called to me. If I listened closely enough to the sound of swaying trees, the wind tossing about crunchy leaves as the birds sat on branches chirping away, I could almost hear a faint voice calling out to me, telling me that it loved me.

I stopped shy of the church, always making sure I never touched the actual land. There was a white fence that cut the church off from the dirt road where I stood. I watched as a few church members entered the church dressed in nice slacks and dress shirts. One woman had on a hat so big I thought she was going to tip over. I was surprised she even made it through the door.

Faith turned around to me with her Bible in her hands and smiled. "See you after church. I'm gonna have lots to teach you."

I frowned and kicked dirt in the air. I didn't want to hear about the Bible anymore if I couldn't learn it by sitting in church myself. I hated how unfair life was. I wished I were Faith. But instead of complaining about it, I just nodded. "Okay, Faith."

I watched her walk onto the church grounds. She turned around to me just before she entered the church and blew me a kiss. I caught it in my hands and continued walking to my favorite spot on Sunday mornings, where I pretended to be a part of something I was not.

Chapter 3

Once me and Faith were fifteen and old enough to watch ourselves, Momma would start going into the city on the weekends doing God knows what with God knows who. She seemed happy when she came home; Faith was the first to suspect that it was because of a man.

Whenever Momma left, I was the first to want to act up. I would call boys over to the house and flirt while Faith stayed in her room, reading her Bible.

I loved the attention I got from boys and men. Momma was right when she said around sixteen I'd look like a woman and many men would try to seduce me. Men would come from the city to take advantage of a small-town, naïve girl. I was the first one they wanted and I loved it. I was the duckling who everybody called ugly, but at fifteen, I was praised for my beauty. Nobody wanted to talk to Faith; they said that she was a Jesus freak and wouldn't put out. Well, whatever she wouldn't do, I did. I felt that it was my time to get the attention that I deserved as a little girl.

One weekend when Momma was away, I called up a college boy who played football for South Carolina University. The girls in our high school used to talk about how sexy he was and I had to have what they didn't have. He actually spotted me one day, walking home from school. He pulled up in a nice all-black BMW with the brightest smile. He looked cool and mysterious in those dark sunglasses and had my attention immediately.

"What's good?" he asked.

I looked behind at the other girls he had passed and felt special that he stopped for me. Momma said any man would stop for a girl who had a butt like mine. I used it to my advantage. I leaned on his door, poking my butt out in the air to let the girls behind me know that I was flirting, in case they tried to talk to him.

"Hey, baby, just walking home from school."

He nodded. "Need a ride?"

Did I? Well, I had two options: either I seem easy and get in his car and show off in front of those girls, or I play hard to get and keep on walking. Eventually he would pull back up beside me and ask for my number, and I would give it to him. I decided to go with my second choice.

"I like to walk. It keeps my figure nice."

I didn't have to see his eyes to know that he was admiring my body. They all did. I turned around and started switching my hips on down the road. Seconds later, he pulled up beside me. I smiled inside.

"Dang, ma. No love? I'm just trying to be a good old-fashioned gentleman."

"Well if you were a true gentleman, you would've offered those girls back there a ride home too."

He smiled. "Oh, you're feisty. I like that. How old are you?"

"Seventeen," I lied. He was around twenty years old; if he knew that I was fifteen, I'd hear his tires burn and he'd speed away. I lived by the motto of "what he don't know won't hurt!"

"I want to get to know you."

"I bet you do, Mr. No Name."

He smiled. "Call me Daune, and what's your name?"

"You can call me cutie for now."

"Okay, cutie." He laughed. "So am I giving you a ride or not?"

"No."

"Well can I get your number?" He handed me his phone and I saved my number.

"It's saved under cutie number two, because you already got a cutie listed in your contacts." I rolled my eyes. "But call me, maybe," I said as I walked away. I heard his tires screech and smelled burning rubber as he hurriedly pulled off. *Show-off.*

I saw Momma pacing on the front porch as I approached. Her hair was wrapped in a blue scarf and she was still in her nightclothes. When she saw me, she gave me the evil eye. "Get your fast behind inside!" Momma shouted in an intimidating voice. She no longer scared me the way she did when I was young and helpless so I took my good old time walking up to the porch. The worst she could do was smack me, and I was immune to those smacks. "I ain't got all day to wait on you, child! Get to steppin'!"

"Fine, Momma, dang!" I yelled back, slowly walking up the porch steps. When I reached the top step, Momma grabbed me by the hair and yanked me inside.

"Yeah, word travels fast in this small town, honey. I got a call from Ms. Francine saying she saw you out her window talkin' to some hot boy in a Benz."

"It was a BMW."

Momma smacked me across the face for correcting her. I didn't even flinch.

"I don't care what kind of a car it was, honey, any boy old enough to drive it is too old for you." Momma shook her head and let go of my hair. "And I heard you was bending over like a ho! You a ho now?"

"No, Momma. I bent over so that I could hear him," I lied. "He said he was lost and needed directions so I gave it to him. You always wanna listen to all the he-say/she-say and never to me."

"Because you lie. You been lying since the day you was born!"

"How am I gonna lie if I can't talk?"

Momma smacked me again. I kept my eyes even with hers.

"I'm 'bout sick of you talking back to me like you grown. Last time I checked, you ain't nothing but a little girl. Go on, though. Keep thinking you grown. If you end up pregnant, I'm kicking you out. Remember that." She walked off into the kitchen, mumbling under her breath.

I sighed, tossed my book bag on the ground, and went to my room. Faith was the good girl. Every day after school, she would go down to the middle school and tutor children. She didn't have time to worry about boys because she stayed in her books. She always had something to say about my behavior, though.

When she came home, she headed straight to my room and locked the door behind her. I had just gotten off the phone with one of my friends from school. I rolled my eyes when I saw her. "Can you knock?"

"Who was that boy you were talking to on the way home from school?" She was upset, which was her normal. Lately, I always did something stupid to make her angry.

"Let me guess." I rolled over to face her. "Momma told you."

"No, one of the tutors who goes to our school told me. Answer the question."

"Oh you know, just one of the many men who want me. His name was Daune and he drives a BMW. I bet he got a lot of money."

"Hope, who cares about money?"

"Um, me!"

"The Bible says we shouldn't worship idols."

I covered my face, trying to hide my irritation. "Who cares about your Bible? Never did me any good."

"Maybe because you don't read it!"

"I don't read it because I don't have one!"

"Borrow mine!"

"Borrow the Bible that Grandma got you? Where's my Bible? She didn't give me one." I sighed. "Faith, I'm tired of living through you, borrowing your stuff, listening to stories about Jesus through you. Nobody gave me the chance to learn it for myself and I'm at the age now where I couldn't care less. If you give me that Bible, I'll burn it."

Faith stepped back as if smacked. It made me laugh. Faith had never gotten smacked a day in her life and I almost hated her for it. Almost.

"Hope—"

"Faith, can you please get out of my room?"

She nodded slowly and let me be.

Faith and I barely said a word to each other that next day; that was, until Momma came barging into the house with a man. A fine man at that. Faith was in the kitchen cleaning while I sat lazily on the couch watching old reruns and talking on the phone. Our house wasn't much, but we made due. We had a small living room with an old orange couch, a blue chair, and a small TV. Momma hung pictures of Faith in her pretty dresses all around the house. The kitchen was barely big enough for two people due to the table that sat in the middle, and most of the time the cabinets and refrigerator were empty. Momma did have three bedrooms, though. Faith's room was right next to mine, and there was a small door in the wall that allowed us to go back and forth from room to room. It came in handy on nights where the storms were too loud. My bedroom was plain, with a bed and a dresser. Faith was more of a girly girl and had to have dolls decorating every corner of her room. I thought she was too old but Momma insisted. It was Faith's room Momma showed off whenever she had company.

I was sitting in the living room, bored from watching TV, and decided to go outside. Just as I reached the door, Momma swung it open, knocking me to the floor.

"Hey, girls!" she said happily, oblivious to knocking me over. I noticed a pair of slick black dress shoes behind her. My eyes passed his shoes, glanced at his trousers, continued up to his blazer, and landed on his lips. This man had to be only thirty years old and smiled like Morris Chestnut. It was obvious that even under that black blazer he was packing some tasty muscles.

I shook the idea of his body out of my mind and stood up, putting up my normal wall filled with attitude. Momma came to me and hugged me kindly. It took me more by surprise than getting knocked over by the door.

"Hope! My beautiful daughter. Where's your sister?"

"I'm in the kitchen cooking, Momma!" Faith's voice echoed throughout the house.

I couldn't believe Momma had called me beautiful; she always saved those kinds of words for Faith. I was going to touch my face to see if something had changed; but, instead, I put my hands on my hips and eyed the man who smiled back at me. The fact that Momma had called me beautiful was now a distant memory. It didn't count if Momma only said it to impress him.

"Who is this man?" I asked with an obvious attitude.

Momma turned around to the man and smiled. "She's the feisty one I was telling you about."

He smiled at me, blazing those perfect white teeth. "Hope, right? Hi, I'm John, you're mom's boyfriend," he stated, sounding proper and prim.

Boyfriend? And I didn't know about him?

I was always known for my dramatic moments. I kicked John in his leg and ran up the porch steps in a fit. I heard John curse loudly and Momma yelled at me, but I didn't care. She would smack me later, I knew that much, but to me it was worth it. Momma brought a stranger home, a man neither Faith nor I knew about. She deserved to be smacked, and since I couldn't smack my own mother, I kicked her boyfriend.

I stayed in my bedroom for about an hour, listening through the door as Faith buttered up to John. I bet Momma was proud. Leave it to Faith to save the day I probably ruined.

Momma frowned when she saw me enter into the living room. Faith and Momma's boyfriend looked up as well, but their nonchalant expressions told me they had forgotten about the kick. "Now that you're done having one of your moments, come help us carry John's things into my room."

I followed John outside and watched as he began struggling with some luggage near his car. I turned to Momma as she and Faith came from inside of the house and stood on the porch.

"Why he got so much luggage?" I asked, still holding strong to my attitude.

Momma ignored my question and went to help John with the rest of the luggage. When she passed me on the step, she purposely bumped in to me. I heard a thump when she set the luggage down inside of the house.

I turned to Faith. "Is she moving that man in our house?" Faith only nodded, sourly. "What? No! We don't even know him!" And it was true. Not only did Momma bring a stranger home, she was moving him in with us. I couldn't believe Faith was just standing there, accepting it with just a sour expression.

Furious, I walked up to John with my hands on my hips. He was still busy retrieving the rest of his bags from the trunk and hadn't noticed me. I bet another kick to his leg would get his attention.

"And how long have you known my momma?" I asked, fighting back the urge to attack him.

He turned around with a smooth smile. How could he be so nice after I kicked him? "Awhile now, why?"

"Because she never said anything about a man."

He wiped the sweat from his forehead with the back of his hand. The afternoon sun seemed to be getting to him. "That's because your mother is a grown woman and doesn't have to tell you kids everything."

"A grown woman don't bring a stranger around her teenage girls," I spat.

"Well, I assure you, I'm no stranger."

"You talk like a white person."

"I'm educated."

"You went to college?"

"Yes."

"Jail?"

John laughed. "No, and I don't ever plan on it. You always ask this many questions?"

"I need to, especially if you think you just about to come up in my house and lie in my momma's bed and do the nasty. I don't know you and I darn sure don't want to. You can take all your luggage and shove it up your—"

"Hope!" Momma called from the porch. I was so consumed by my argument that I didn't notice she came from the house again. "Hurry up and bring his bags in the house." She then looked to her boyfriend. "Is she harassing you, John?"

John gave me a measured look and then shook his head. "No, we are getting along just fine." He smiled at me once more before joining my momma in the house. And I stood there, near his car, angry that I had no authority to make him leave. I couldn't believe my own momma would move a man in without first introducing him to both Faith and me beforehand. I could already tell I wasn't going to like John. Had I known then what I know now, I would've done anything to make sure he didn't enter that house.

Chapter 4

I was afraid that John would treat my momma wrong. I heard too many stories about abusive, drunken men. As much as I hated my momma, I loved her enough to only want the best for her. John had been staying with us for a month and seemed to make Momma happy, so I slowly began to accept him as an addition to our house.

Momma seemed happier with him around. She was always walking around the house, humming and cleaning. Treating me just like my sister. Being the mom she should've been from day one. I didn't buy it. Soon the honeymoon phase of her relationship would die down, she'd no longer be as happy, and would return to her usual bitter ways. I kept myself prepared. Faith, on the other hand, was too naïve, and fell right into the trap from day one. I couldn't blame her. We seemed like a family for once. A real, good family.

Most of the time, John was working at a bank. He came home around seven, just in time for dinner, and would amuse us with his eventful day. We all would sit around the dinner table and laugh. John was good at making people feel at ease with him.

"So, how's school, Hope?" he asked, gravely interested. I was taken by surprise at the fact that he had asked me and not Faith. I was used to everyone giving Faith all of the attention. John was different. He tried harder with me, because he knew how differently Momma treated Faith and me, and he would always try to balance it out by showing me more attention. I also believed he just wanted my approval.

"Um." I swallowed a huge bite of spaghetti. "School's okay."

"I got an A on my math test," Faith exclaimed.

I almost choked on another forkful of spaghetti. Leave it up to Faith to brag and turn all heads toward her. I was sure John was going to congratulate her but his eyes stayed focused on me.

"And you, Hope? What grade did you get?"

I eyed John quizzically. "I got a D."

"Why?" he asked.

"Because math is my weakest subject." I sighed.

I heard Momma's fork drop on her plate. "Hope, now what I tell you about them grades? I'm 'bout tired of you failing every class. You—"

"Juanita, let me handle this," John said calmly as he looked at Momma. He watched her as if waiting for her to continue overreacting, and when she didn't, he continued. "Hope, are all of your grades bad?"

"No," I said. I didn't consider C to be a bad grade.

"What's your favorite class?"

That was easy. "Choir."

"You like to sing?"

I nodded.

"How about this, if you get that math grade up to a C, I'll take you and your sister to a concert in the city."

Our eyes lit up. "Really?" I asked.

He nodded. "I am a man of my word."

I looked to Momma for approval and she reluctantly nodded. I jumped up from my seat in excitement. "John, thank you! This is the bomb! I ain't never been to a concert before and I always wanted to go. I want to perform on stage in front of millions one day, like Mariah Carey. I promise I'll get my grades up. I'll make it a B!"

John smiled at my momma and pointed his fork in her direction. "You got to give them motivation. Yelling and screaming at them won't help a thing."

And he was right. A month later, I brought my grade up to a B and John took us to go see Mariah Carey live. It was one of the best moments of my childhood. That day, I really began to admire the man who walked into all of our lives.

When the winter came, so did the cold that threatened all of our sanity. And I don't mean the kind of cold that makes a person turn their heat up; this was a cold that came from the mind and, if not contained, could devour the body. John had now been around for five months and I noticed Momma's edge coming back. Their honeymoon phase was definitely over. John and Momma started to argue a lot about some of the stupidest things.

John and I were in a middle of playing a card game on the floor when Momma burst through the front door, hot and heavy and ready to attack. My heart stopped. I ran through all the things I did in the past week that would upset her. I had finally got into a fight with Dee Dee, Jordan's sister; I had stolen some donuts from the corner store; and I kissed a boy behind the high school. Did anyone see these things? I had made sure to be careful.

Momma's eyes skipped over me and settled on John. She burned holes into him. "John, what's the real reason you moved out here to the country?"

He froze. "Because I wanted to be with you."

"You got one more time to lie to me." Momma pointed a firm finger at John and took another step toward him. "Why did you move out here to the country?"

John swallowed hard and stood up slowly. "Because I love you."

Momma screamed and lunged at John, swinging wildly. "I heard about your gambling problem! I know you fled the city so that they wouldn't kill you! You don't love me. You're using me!" She further explained that a man came up to her, showing her a picture of John, and told her that he was looking for John Davis, who owed him money. Said rumor had it that John was hiding out in our part of the country until things blew over.

"Baby, I promise!" John said while pushing Momma against the wall. He had both of her hands pinned against the wall and was struggling to contain her. "Yes, I got into some trouble, but that was after you asked me to move in with you. That's not why I'm here!"

Momma pushed herself away from him. "You won't lie to me. Get out of my house."

John's eyes focused on me. They were so pleading. He was silently begging for me to believe him. And I did. I loved John. It took months, but once I trusted him, once I saw his dedication to me, I flocked to him. I had never had a daddy or any man love me like John did.

"Momma, please," I begged. "Don't make him go. Please!"

"Hope . . ." She looked at me, her eyes a raging fire. She shook her head and then turned toward the hallway. "Faith!" she screamed out and waited for Faith to come into the room. "Go pack his clothes and sit them on the porch." Faith looked from Momma, to John, and then to me. I could see the worry lines etched in her forehead but she didn't dare ask what was going on. Faith simply nodded but she didn't move. Momma returned her attention to John. "You can come get your stuff in the morning but I want you gone. Now!"

"Momma, no!" I ran to John and wrapped my arms around him. My tears stole my vision, but I only hugged John tighter. "Don't make him leave!"

John's hands found my hair and caressed me softly. "It's okay, baby."

"No, it's not!" I yelled, clinging tighter to his torso. I tried everything I could to make it hard for him to walk as he started to head toward the door. "John, don't go! Please, I'll talk to Momma. I'll make her listen."

I looked at Faith, my eyes begging hers for help, but she just stood in the kitchen doorway; she hadn't moved or said a word. I hated her for just standing there. I hated that she didn't love John like I did. He was the glue that mended my happiness. He was the only thing that kept Momma from mistreating me. How could Faith stand there and not come to his defense?

John managed get out of the house and down the porch steps with me tugging and pulling him back to the house. He pried my hands from his shirt and gently pushed me away. "You're making this harder, Hope. Stop acting like a child. You're fifteen!" he said.

"John, don't leave me!" I cried, clinging to his shirt. He sighed and wiped the snot from my nose with a handkerchief and kissed my cheek. "John, if you leave, who's gonna love me?"

I struck a nerve and watched as a single tear paved a line down his face. He took my face into his hands and said, "Your sister will love you."

I shook my head. "She's too consumed in her Bible to worry about me like she used to when we were kids."

"Your momma wi—"

"She only loves Faith."

John sighed but he wore an expression of determination. "Hope, I am a man of my word. Do you remember when I took you and your sister to that concert? Have I ever lied to you?" I shook my head. "Then believe me when I tell you this, I will be back. Give your momma time to calm down and think things through. Give it two weeks. I'll be back. I promise."

"How do you know?"

John smiled. "Because when a woman loves, she loves." He let go of my face and got into his car.

I watched him drive away, holding on to that promise.

I slowly walked back up to the house, knowing that Momma was ready to take all of her anger out on me for taking John's side. I didn't care. I'd welcome her slap across my face or the punch to my stomach. It was a distraction from the pain I felt inside.

"How dare you pick his side over mine? I'm your momma!" She stormed toward me, smacking me back against the front door. "Go in my room and start helping your sister pack his stuff. And no dinner for you. Go to bed hungry and miserable for all I care."

Faith already had half of John's things packed away when I entered Momma's room. She froze when she saw my swollen cheek. I felt her condolences through unspoken words. I sat beside her and finished packing his stuff. I hid one of his shirts under my momma's bed and made a mental note to come back for it. I needed something to remember him by in case Momma didn't take him back. Faith once told me that only God keeps true to His word.

The next week was hell. Momma started drinking the moonshine our neighbors made, and would come home in a drunken fit, yelling at me for no reason at all. One night, as I sat watching TV with Faith, Momma came stumbling into the house with a long bag. I could already tell there was a dress inside of it. And obviously so could Faith, because she jumped off of the couch immediately.

"Momma, what is that?" she asked as Momma clumsily shut the door behind her.

"I bought you a dress," she slurred. "For homecoming."

"Homecoming?" I frowned. "She don't got a date!"

"Yeah, she does, and mind your business!" Momma yelled. "She going with Jordan."

I almost threw up. "What? Faith, you know I hate him!"

"Well, Jordan gonna be a big basketball player one day and I want at least one of my daughters to be well off." Momma's words stung but I didn't show the hurt that I felt. "Me and his momma got to talkin' and started arrangin' everything!"

Faith was oblivious to my hurt. She started ripping the bag away from the dress and held it in the air. It was a beautiful pink dress with multicolored rhinestones embedded in the waistline. The bottom of the dress was form fitting and was long enough to create a train that flowed behind her as she walked. It was by far the most beautiful dress I'd seen. Momma had to have paid a fortune for it, most likely the electric bill money.

"Where's my dress?" I felt silly to even ask.

"You got a date? No! So you don't get a dress."

"Well, what if I got a date to homecoming?" I asked.

Momma laughed as if I'd said something stupid. "Girl, I told you that you can't date until you're eighteen."

"And you told Faith she can't date until she's sixteen! It's not fair!"

"Well, she gonna marry Jordan one day, and y'all gonna be sixteen in a few weeks. Why are you even questioning me?" Momma asked. "Get out of my presence. You disturb me."

"Fine." I stumped back into my bedroom and slammed my door.

If Momma hadn't been preoccupied with Faith, she would've charged into my room and choked me for slamming doors in her house. I wanted to cry because her words hurt so badly. It was a poison that I unwillingly had to swallow. My stomach churned due to the side effects. I missed John. He would've bought us both a dress. The thought of him being gone brought tears to my eyes. Only a week had past but I was counting down the days until

Momma changed her mind about him. Somehow I blamed myself for him leaving even though it had nothing to do with me. I was so used to everything being blamed on me; it was almost natural to self-loathe.

Faith came into my room a half hour later with her dress on. It fit perfectly on her small frame. As she spun around my room, the light reflected off of the rhinestones, making her look magical. I wanted to hate her for being the favorite, even though it wasn't her fault.

"It's beautiful," she said. Her smile quickly turned into a frown. "But I'm gonna tell Momma to take it back."

"Why? You deserve it." I smiled, but it didn't meet my eyes.

"And you don't? Hope, when we were younger we couldn't stand up for ourselves. We didn't know how to tell Momma that she was wrong! But now we can. I ain't accepting another gift from her unless she gets you one too."

"Faith, I'm used to it. It don't faze me no more," I lied. The truth was I was crushed. It opened old scars that never healed properly. "Plus I ain't never wore a dress a day in my life and I ain't 'bout to start wearing one now."

"Are you sure?" she asked. "I don't wanna go without you."

"You got Jordan."

She tried to hold back a smile. I knew she liked him deep down. There was nothing I could do about it.

"I do. Oh, I feel so special!" she said, twirling around the room again. "I'm gonna go change before I get it dirty."

The cold around me returned once she left the room. I let my tears fall freely but held a pillow over my head so that no one could hear me cry. I wanted to run away, have a rich family with no kids adopt me, and buy me all the dresses my heart desired. I wanted to go to homecoming and dance. I wanted to be free.

All my life I was told I was the bad twin, the rotten one. I had so much anger sitting at the bottom of my heart, slowly rising. I envied my sister and hated my mother. If they thought I was bad as a child, they hadn't seen a thing. I'd show all of them how bad a girl could get. I'd be ruthless. A girl who no longer cared. I'd treat everyone as badly as I had been treated and I'd blame it all on Momma. She'd created a monster.

Once Momma and Faith fell asleep, I snuck into Faith's room and took her dress. I slowly opened her window and climbed out of her room. I wanted her to think someone had snuck in and stolen it. Maybe I was wrong for doing it, but I felt they owed me that dress. I walked a few miles down the dark street until I saw headlights. Once the car was close enough, I started waving my arms.

The car slowed down beside me. A white man with half his teeth missing smiled at me. "What you doin' out here at one in the mornin'?"

"I got lost. I need a ride into the city," I told him. "I got this expensive dress that I can give you, it's Vera Wang."

"Hot diggity!" he exclaimed. "I'll ride you to the border and back for that dress. You got any idea how much that dress costs?"

I got into his car and set the dress on my lap. "I don't know and I don't care. It's yours."

He smiled and sped off.

An hour later we were in the city. The bright lights shined beautifully in the night sky. I marveled out of the window as we passed houses and buildings. We were in the heart of city. People were still out, walking about as if it were still daytime. I noticed a line of people in skimpy clothes waiting to get inside of a club called Fire. I memorized everything about the building, hoping one day I'd be able to go to a place like that.

The man pulled up to the curb. "Where do you want me to take you?"

I thought about the bank John worked at and remembered him telling me it was the largest bank downtown. I turned to the old man. "Can you take me to National Bank? The big one downtown?"

"It's right around the corner," he grunted, and pushed on the gas.

A few minutes later, we were sitting in front of a black skyscraper with a big sign that read NATIONAL BANK. I got out of the car and thanked the man. I watched as he drove off.

It was two in the morning and chilly out. I would have to wait outside the building all night until John came in to work. I had no plan. I remember thinking, *What will I say to him? Come home?* He probably would freak out before I got the chance to explain why I was there. I doubted it would change a thing.

I spent that whole night sitting by the building, wondering if my plan to get him home would work. Around five, I dozed off, but was quickly awakened when the first employee showed up to open the bank. It was a middle-aged Asian man with short black hair and a small frame. The man looked down at me with furrowed brows. "Did you sleep out here all night?"

"Yeah," I said. "Does John Davis still work here?"

"He'll be in around ten. Are you his family?"

I nodded. "Yeah."

"Come inside, we'll get you something to drink. There's a lobby on the third floor. You can rest there until he comes in. I'll let him know you're up here as soon as he walks in."

"Thanks."

I found my way up to the lobby and nestled into a chair and dozed off. I dreamed about fame and fortune and everyone loving me. I dreamed of singing at Madison Square Garden in front of millions, hearing them chant my name. Yes, they'd all chant my name. They got louder, they kept chanting.

"Hope!" I was startled awake. John stood over me, looking ten years older from stress. "Hope, wake up! What are you doing here? Did something happen? Is your mom okay? Faith, is she—"

"She's fine, they're both fine." I was so happy to see him. I immediately jumped into his arms, forcing him into a seat, crushing him. "John, I missed you. Come home!"

"Did you come all the way to my job to tell me this?"

"No." I shook my head, remembering my lie. I worked up some fake tears and noticed how John's face softened. "We got robbed." I shuddered. "Somebody snuck in Faith's room while she was sleeping and took some of her things. I heard them leave through her window and ran outside to see what was going on. The man had her new dress and so I tried to fight him but he grabbed me and threw me in his car. I was so scared, John!"

"How did you get away?"

"He rode into the city and kicked me out of his car and kept going. I was only a few blocks away from your job. I remembered you worked in the biggest bank downtown and asked some people for directions and I ended up here. John, we need you to come home!" I cried.

John nodded once and stood up. "Come on, I'm taking you home."

John didn't say a word to me on the way home. I didn't expect him to. Most likely he was blaming himself for letting this happen. If he had been there, he would've killed the intruder and I'd still be safe at home. I hated that my lie was eating away at him, but I had no choice. I would do anything I needed to, to bring that little piece of happiness back into my life.

John pulled up in the driveway. Momma was already sitting out on the porch looking slightly worried. Her face hardened when she saw him. She noticed me in the passenger seat and stood up.

"Faith!" she called.

Faith came to the door as John and I got out of the car. Faith immediately ran down the steps and threw herself into my arms, crying. "Hope, I was so scared! My window was opened and my dress was missing and so were you!"

Momma walked to the edge of the porch with her arms folded. "Hope, what did you do with that girl's dress, and why did you bring him here?"

I looked to John for reassurance. I needed to know that he was there to help and protect me if things got ugly. He nodded, sending me a wave of encouragement.

"Momma, somebody came in through Faith's window and stole her dress. I heard them by my bedroom window and ran outside. I stopped him before he could come into my room but he snatched me up, rode into the city, and dumped me on the street!"

I expected my momma to react differently, but all she said was, "You dumber than you look, Hope. And that still don't explain why the hell this man is in my yard with that sad puppy face!"

"She came to my job, Juanita. She didn't have anywhere else to go," John explained.

"She should've walked her black butt home!" Momma told him.

"Momma, this wouldn't have happened if John was still here!"

Momma lowered her eyes at me. "You think you slick, trying to make me feel guilty for kicking him out?"

I shook my head. "No, Momma. It's the truth. The man is supposed to be the protector."

"Juanita, what if somebody would've killed Hope?" Momma frowned but didn't really seem affected by what John had said until he continued. "What if they would've killed Faith?"

Momma stepped back and looked at the both of us but her eyes lingered on Faith. Of course, Momma reacted like a mother when he mentioned Faith. John walked slowly toward my momma with his hands out, pleading. "I don't care if you don't ever want to touch me again, Juanita. But let's make it work for the kids. Let's think about them." He was now standing directly in front of Momma. She thought for a moment and then nodded.

"Well heck. I s'pose you're right." Momma finally smiled. "I missed you."

"I missed you too." John brought her into his arms.

My plan worked. I brought John back home and it was the happiest day of my life.

Chapter 5

Things went back to how they were. It did take a few days for Momma's anger toward John to vanish, but once it did, she was singing around the house again. I loved her voice. It sounded a lot like mine when I would sing. Momma told me that when I was a little girl, I would sing so loud the neighborhood could hear me. And then she said I had a big mouth and that singing wasn't going to get me anywhere in life. She told me to keep my head in the books like Faith. Everything I did was compared to Faith.

"Why don't you be polite like Faith?"

"Faith is such a good girl, why can't you be like your sister?"

"Everyone says they love Faith. Why you gotta be so unlovable?"

"Faith looks just like an angel. You should look more like Faith."

I spent many years wondering why I couldn't be like Faith. I used to follow her around the house trying to walk like she did. I watched the way her mouth moved when she talked. I tried to put my hair in buns like Faith did, but my hair wasn't long enough because it broke off from Momma's neglect. She never took care of my hair the way she did with Faith. Once when I was younger, I cut Faith's hair off when she was sleeping and put it on my hair. I finally had a bun. I ran out to Momma to show her what I did, to let her know that I was finally pretty, like Faith. I had never gotten beaten so badly in my life. Of course Faith's hair grew back, but my self-image never did.

One day, I decided to stop trying to be my perfect sister. I'd cringe anytime someone mentioned her name. I didn't want any comparison to her. I started to distance myself, barely saying a word, keeping myself locked up in my bedroom. I could tell that she was hurt by it, but I didn't care. I'd felt pain my whole life; she could handle it too. That's when Faith started to focus more and more on church. After school, she went to the middle school to go tutor for free. On Sundays, she'd stay longer at church to help out with whatever she could. When we did see each other, we barely spoke. When I distanced myself from her, it only hurt me worse. I thought being mean to her would satisfy me, but it only made me angrier. If John hadn't come into our lives, Lord knows what I would've done once I finally exploded.

I admired John. It was innocent. I'd sit in the kitchen and watch him make breakfast. I was fascinated whenever he shaved. I'd sit on the sink and watch in awe. One time, he took the shaving cream and squirted it all over my face. I retaliated by squirting toothpaste in his hair. Momma came barging into the bathroom when she heard all the ruckus. When she left, John and I cracked up and continued our bathroom war.

John was closer to me than he was with Faith, partly because I demanded all of his attention. Faith couldn't have him. He was mine. I was the one who brought him back after Momma broke up with him. Nobody else accomplished it. I was somewhat possessive over John. I had never known what it was like to have a father figure, to have a man tell me that he loved me. I bathed in the attention that he showed me. He was the only person who was able to brighten the dark spots in my life.

One night, I burst into Faith's room and locked the door behind me. I was bursting at the seams with excitement. I had talked to one of my male friends at school who said one of his cousins was having a house party in the city. Faith and I had never been to a house party before and I thought she'd be as thrilled as I was.

"House party?" Faith's mouth dropped open after I told her of my plans. "And in the city? No. There's gonna be a lot of crazy boys looking to prey on freshmen like us! No! I'm not going!"

"Stop being a Bible hugger and live for once."

"I can breathe, I can eat, I can walk, I can see. That's living," she said.

"Faith, we gonna be sixteen in a few days, let's party!"

"No."

"Jesus went to parties."

"Not the same kind of party you're talking about!" Faith screamed. She would get so angry whenever people were blasphemous. It made me laugh. "It's not funny."

"Fine, Faith. Don't go. Waste away your life. Just tell Mom that I'm sick and not to bother me."

"So you're still going?"

"Heck yeah, regardless. I have a ride. What can go wrong?"

Faith's face squinted up, which was what she did whenever battling a demon, as she called it. "Fine."

"Fine, what?"

"I'll go. But only because I want to make sure you're okay."

I jumped up and down in excitement.

Later that day, we pulled up to the party in a beat-down Cadillac that was two seconds from breaking down. It belonged to Mike, a friend of ours from school. He agreed to let us ride with him to the party. I got out of the car feeling sexy. I had tied my shirt in the back to show off my stomach. I drew a little heart just above my waistline. I cut some old, tight-fitting jeans into some booty shorts and cleaned my gym shoes until they looked brand new. Momma had bought a knock-off Chanel purse, and it hung from my shoulder. Faith, on the other hand, had on an unflattering, long flowered dress, no makeup, and a bun. She didn't look fit for a party.

I headed to the door with Faith trailing shyly behind me. A few girls were on the side of us, walking up to the party. They all had their noses turned up at me. It made me smile; it meant I was doing something right.

I walked into the party and was greeted by loud music blasting from the speakers. Two dozen people were crowded into the living room, dancing; a few couples leaned against the wall, talking or making out; and a bunch of boys were drinking liquor and partying in the kitchen. I decided that was where I wanted to be.

"I'm going to the kitchen. Just sit on the couch or something," I yelled to Faith over the music. I watched her hesitantly walk over to the couch and sit by a couple making out. I wanted to laugh at her expression.

I headed for the kitchen, glowing with confidence. I was looking good, my weave was flowing down my back, and my butt looked even bigger in the tight shorts. I noticed every head that turned in my direction. It was me they were looking at, not Faith. Me.

"What's good, cutie?" one of the boys asked as I walked into the kitchen. He was the cutest one with long dreads and a bright grill. He looked like he had money. "What you drinkin' on?"

"Give me whatever you got."

The guys laughed. "So if I give you one hundred proof liquor, you'd down it?"

I rolled my eyes. "Like I said, I'll drink whatever you got."

He smiled. "I like you already, sexy." He poured me a shot of liquor. "Drink up."

I took the glass from his hands and swallowed the liquor. I tried my hardest not to make a face as it burned down my throat. I slammed the shot down on the countertop. "Give me another one."

His eyes widened as if impressed and gave his friends a look. "Shorty mean!"

"Ay, and she got a fatty!" one of the ugly ones called from behind me. I smiled and turned around for him to see.

"Dang, they don't breed 'em like this except down South. Thin waist, big butt, long hair . . . And I don't care if it's weave! I bet I'll still pull on it," he said to his friends, who agreed in unison. He handed me my second shot.

I stared deeply into his dark eyes and slowly raised the shot glass to my lips. I wanted to play with him, keep him watching my every move, make him want me. He licked his lips and the liquor went down. I looked around, noticing that they were all looking at me like they wanted to devour me. It made me feel so good.

"Oh!" I said, recognizing the song that came on. "This is my jam! Come dance with me!" I grabbed his hand and pulled him into the living room. I noticed I was slightly off balance, but I felt good inside. I had no worries.

I started grinding on him slowly and built my way up into the beat. I grabbed his arms and wrapped them around my waist. I glanced over at Faith; her look was of pure disapproval, which was normal for her. Nothing I did was up to her "Christian" expectations. But I didn't live to please her or my mother at that time, and especially not God. It was finally my time to feel happy.

I turned around to face the boy with a smile. "You want a private dance?" I asked.

"Yeah, we can go to my room."

"You live here?" I asked, surprised. He only nodded and quickly pulled me along. I didn't look to see Faith's expression; I already knew. Another disappointment.

We kissed on the way up the stairs, tugging at each other's clothing, me moving away and laughing whenever he tried to take anything off. He kicked open his bedroom door and cut the light on. His room was simple, but it matched his personality. He had a king-sized bed with red silk sheets and a few posters of rappers on either wall. He walked over to his bed and sat down, watching my every move. He didn't have to say a word for me to know what he wanted. I shut the door behind me and began to dance.

"Naw, don't dance. Come here."

"But I thought you wanted a dance."

"Just come here," he said, and I obeyed. I took a seat next to him, suddenly feeling very conscious of myself. It was the first time that I was alone in a room with a boy.

He put his hands on my leg and slowly started trailing circles up my thigh. I shifted and grabbed his hand and kissed it. I didn't want him touching me in that way. I thought he only wanted a dance. Suddenly, he pushed me back on the bed and climbed on top of me. He was careful not to crush me with his weight.

"How old are you?" he asked.

I could've lied, but I didn't want to. Not in such a heavy situation in which I had no experience. I said, "Fifteen."

He smiled and started kissing my neck. "Old enough. You a virgin?"

"Yes," I said, trying to push him off of me. I wasn't ready for what he had in mind. The room started spinning around me. I tried to focus on the ceiling above, but I couldn't. My stomach started turning. I was going to be sick. "Move."

"Naw," he said, pushing down on me. He started unbuckling his pants and parted my legs. His hands found my zipper and he began tugging at it.

"Please." I covered my mouth. I couldn't hold it down and I didn't want to be in this situation. It was going too far. I wasn't ready. Stupid of me to go into a room with a boy and think the only thing he wanted was a dance.

"I said no!"

He slid his hands inside of my shorts. I tried to move his hands, but he was too strong. He slid my shorts down to my knees.

"Stop!" I closed my eyes. I felt the vomit come up my throat and I threw up, spitting bile all over the place.

"Did you just throw up on me?" he asked incredulously.

My eyes focused on him, watching as he jumped off the bed covered in my vomit. He took his shirt off, threw it on the ground, and ran into his bathroom. I didn't feel bad; in fact, I laughed all the way to his bedroom door and stumbled to the stairs. I heard shouting below and the music abruptly stopped.

"Police!"

I silently cursed and stumbled down the stairs. All around me was chaos. The front door was busted open. A few police men were standing around, checking cups for alcohol, trying to catch drunken kids, assessing the situation. Half of the house had emptied through the back door and a few kids were still running around, trying to find their friends.

Faith.

My heart dropped. *Where did she go?* I hit the last step and started to panic. I had a few seconds to grab her before the police got me. I ran to the bathroom, which was empty. I looked in the kitchen, but a police officer was standing in there, testing the punch. He turned around and saw me standing there. I quickly ran away.

"Hey!" he shouted. "Get back here!"

It was too late. *Faith must've run outside with the rest of the kids.* I needed to find her. I felt so regretful, wishing I hadn't dragged her out here. She hadn't wanted to come. It was all my fault. I ran out the back door, looking for my twin, and ran into a few girls walking away from the party. I stopped them as they were getting into their car.

"Hey, y'all seen a light-skinned chick with a long flowered dress?" They shook their heads and got into the car. Felling hopeless, I ran up to a boy with a red afro. "You seen a light-skinned girl with a flowered dress?" He shook his head no too. I walked around to the front of the house. A few police officers were standing on the porch; one had a dark-skinned boy in handcuffs, escorting him to one of the three police cars. Another police officer stood on the side of the first car, pushing a girl inside. I studied the floral print dress she wore. It was the same as Faith's. My heart stopped.

I ran closer, but stayed far enough away so that I could run if the police tried to question me. I waited for the officer to move away from her door and walk to the driver's side, but even then her face was turned away. I prayed like crazy, hoping that it wasn't Faith. It couldn't be. It wasn't her fault, she hadn't drunk anything, and she'd just sat there all innocent.

"God, she's a good girl, please don't let it be her," I prayed, but even if it wasn't, then where was she? The police car roared to life and pulled off, but just before it drove out of view, I saw the most delicate face turn toward the window. I couldn't believe my eyes.

They had Faith.

It took four hours to walk home. Four long, arduous hours. I spent the time crying and praying, and when I wasn't crying or praying, I was running through all of the things that could've happened to her. Maybe they took her to prison where she'd have to fight to keep her goodies away from raging lesbian prisoners. Maybe she escaped from the police car and ran for it. Maybe they took her to jail and Momma would have to bail her out. Or maybe it wasn't Faith. Maybe someone else had that same hideous dress and looked similar. Regardless of what happened, I was a dead girl walking.

I had been hoping that I'd be able to hitch a ride home, but it was a lonely walk. Only one car passed by and they were headed in the other direction. I had wasted so much time looking for Faith, I missed any opportunity of a ride home. Luckily only one freeway passed our little town, and I knew my way home. If Momma found out, I was dead. Literally. Looking back at life, I now laugh at this situation. It was one of the lesser evils I've committed. I'd relive it one hundred times over the other things I'd face in life.

By the time I reached our front yard, my feet were calloused and swollen and I had sobered up. The sun began to creep up from behind the distant hills, casting an ominous shadow over my house. I could easily sneak into my room and pretend that nothing happened, but something did. Something big. I took two steps into our yard before I saw Momma sitting stoically on the porch. I almost ran back from where I came but decided to get it over with. I slowly began walking toward her.

"Take your time. You better enjoy these last few seconds of your life," she said, still not moving an inch. Dread replaced every atom in my body. She knew, somehow, she knew what happened.

"Momma—"

"Save your words, you're gonna need them to explain to God why you died before your time." She was so serious.

I nodded and wiped an unruly tear from my right eye. I stood before the porch and hesitated.

One . . . two . . . three. I mentally counted each step as I passed them. *Four.* Momma jumped up from her chair and snatched me up before I could get to five.

I stared up into her low, feral eyes. My own were wide with fear. She yanked me into the house where both Faith and John sat. I didn't bother to look at him. I didn't want to see the disappointment in his eyes. I quickly glanced at Faith, who had puffy, tired eyes from crying. She didn't look up at me. She was angry as well. Momma pushed me up against the wall.

"The police showed up at my house at three in the morning with your sister, handcuffed and crying," Momma began. "Said they found her sitting on the couch at a house party. They tested her for alcohol and questioned her motives. Said she started crying about getting dragged to a party she didn't want to go to and that she was just waiting for her chance to get home. The police took pity on her and brought her home. They said next time it happens, she's going to jail.

"I didn't need to hear anything else from Faith. I already knew who put her up to it. Her sister, the devil himself." Momma smacked me across the face. "You think you grown now? You think just because your birthday is tomorrow, you get to go party and be wild?" She grabbed me by my throat and began choking me. "You ain't grown! You a little girl, but since you wanna act grown, I'm gonna whoop your butt like you grown!" She turned her head toward Faith and John. "Faith, go in your room."

"But, Momma—" Faith started.

"Faith!" she yelled at the top of her lungs, startling Faith. "Go. Now!"

Faith slowly stood up and sulked to her room. At least she didn't hate me enough to want my momma to beat me. I looked over at John, who stared back, impassive. I tried to plead with him through my eyes, but if he noticed, he said nothing.

"Wench!" Momma punched me to the ground before I could even see it coming. I felt her forceful kick connect with my stomach, making me spit blood. She grabbed my head and banged it twice on the ground while cursing at me. I thought I heard John shout in the background. I thought Momma shouted back at him as she punched me again and again. I thought. I couldn't hear anything over the loud ringing in my ears. All I knew what that Momma had stopped hitting me. But it was too late. I felt myself starting to pass out from the head blow and I welcomed the escape.

Chapter 6

I can always sense a storm without looking into the sky. Nature has a way of warning us before a catastrophe, kind of like our own instincts. We can just feel the tension in the air, a black omen waiting to claim its prize. If we're smart and listen to warnings of a storm, we can take shelter before the worst hits. I never had the kind of shelter that protected me whenever life's storm passed. I just stood there, getting drenched by my own sin and tears, and waited for the worst to pass.

When Faith's and my birthday rolled around, I didn't even expect a happy birthday. Too many birthdays passed by without even the slightest acknowledgment from my mother. Faith, on the other hand, was showered with gifts. A pretty new dress, a new comforter set for her bedroom, and sometimes jewelry. Whenever I asked Momma where my gift was, she'd say I didn't deserve one, that I'd done something bad that week. I'd try to remember what I'd done to make Momma so mad that she wouldn't get me a gift, but I couldn't think of anything. By the time I was twelve, I just stopped asking. I stopped expecting anything from her. I suspected she finally had a reason on our sixteenth birthday.

I limped out of my room, still black and blue from the beating of my life. Faith had told me that Momma would've killed me had John not stopped her. She said Momma tried to fight John but he locked her in her bedroom while he and Faith carried me to my room. I had woken up covered in a light salve with a rag over my head. John had fallen asleep on the floor beside me with a bag of melted ice in his hands. I felt loved. Faith told me that she grew more respect for John after that situation. I loved him even more for it.

I limped into the living room, thinking about John and his good heart, and was taken aback in surprise. John stood a few feet away with a poorly decorated birthday cake in his hand that said SWEET 16. Faith was standing beside him.

"Happy birthday, Hope!" the both of them screamed.

Tears instantly poured from my eyes. It was the first time someone had ever baked me a cake. Faith ran up to me, wrapping her arms around me. "John got us both presents!" My heart skipped as I glanced at the two long identical bags sitting against the couch. Momma was nowhere to be seen. "I was waiting for you to wake up so that we can open them!"

John set the cake down on the table next to Faith's cake. He had baked us both our own cakes. I wanted to break down in happiness. I wasn't used to someone showing me so much affection. I walked over to the gift with my name on it. Faith stood in front of her own, with an eager expression.

"Go ahead." John smiled.

I took no time ripping my present free from the bag until it was fully revealed. My eyes shined in wonder as I looked down at the most beautiful gown I'd ever seen. It was far more beautiful than anything Faith had ever worn.

It was a strapless, knee-length beautiful royal-blue dress with a big, frilly bow that tied around the waist. The bottom half of the dress was a tutu that ruffled intricately. Next to the dress was a box I hadn't noticed that had silver heels detailed with diamonds running along the ankle. Faith's dress was long and pink, much like the one I'd stolen from her, and equally as beautiful.

I turned to John, speechless. How could I thank him? What should a person so far in debt to someone's kindness say? John smiled and nodded. He could see the gratefulness in my eyes. I didn't need to say a thing. I walked up and wrapped my arms around him and cried. I felt Faith behind me as she wrapped her arms around the both of us. All too soon, John let go and held my chin up.

"Hope, I want to talk to you in private."

"Okay," I said, allowing him to guide me away from Faith and outside.

We sat out on the porch, staring at the beautiful South Carolina scenery. A weeping willow tree that sat in our yard was the best part about our land. Its branches hung so low, so sadly, I'd imagine that it wept for a love unrequited, much like my love for Momma. And I too hung low, saddened by events out of my control, burdened by the expectation to be my sister.

"Hope," John started, but then he stopped. He didn't know how to address what I knew that he'd been dying to ask ever since he saw how Momma beat me last night. "Why?"

"I did it because I wanted to be free, for once. I wanted to be normal and go to parties and kick it with people who didn't know me for being the wrong twin."

"That's not what I meant," he said. "Why does your mom do this to you?"

It's something I thought about my whole life but I had never expected anyone to ask me. "I think it's because Momma hates me. She had to raise two kids alone with no help. She always said she wished it was only one of us."

He took in my answer and sat silently for a while. Both of us, just staring out at the morning view. "Why don't you go to church with your sister?"

"Because Momma won't let me go. I don't care anymore though, not anymore." It was a lie. I still cared, very much. "Plus Grandma didn't want to hassle around two kids at the same time. Momma said when I was little I was bad, couldn't sit still, and would catch fits. Grandma ain't want no church folk to see that."

He nodded but his eyebrows were set. It was obvious he didn't agree with them. "How does your mom mistreating you make you feel?"

"I guess it makes me feel bad but I understand why she does some of it. She always has a reason to, I guess."

"No," he said firmly. "No mother ever has a good enough reason to mistreat her child to the point of abuse. It messes up a kid's self-worth, makes it hard for them to deal with life. They grow up confused and unloved, and many of them end up with emotional issues."

"What's that?"

"Emotional issues can range from mild depression to mental disorders. Hope, do you love yourself?"

"I never really thought about it, I guess," I told him.

He shook his head. "I want you to really think about it." He turned to me abruptly; his expression was very serious. "If I were your daddy, I would've never let her treat you like this. When I saw how she beat you like that, knowing it wasn't the first time she did it, I almost killed her. I almost left her."

"Why didn't you?"

"You're the only reason I stayed," he told me, finally relaxing. "I'm gonna tell you something I never told anyone. It's our secret. Okay?"

"Okay," I said, barely containing my excitement. I was on the edge of my chair, anticipating what he was going to say.

He sighed, almost shrinking in his seat. A shadow passed over his face, a memory that didn't want to resurface. He blinked a few times and sighed again. Sweat began dripping down his forehead. His expression was almost childlike as if he were afraid. I knew that pain. I felt it every day.

John reached over and squeezed my hand. "My mom was a crackhead and would leave me for days with my dad, who was an alcoholic. He used to beat and leave me unconscious for days. I'd wake up with my mom passed out beside me, high. When I was five, my dad threw me out of his car. He literally opened my door while driving and pushed me out. The doctors said it was a miracle that I lived. They ended up putting me in foster care and I was eventually adopted by a wealthy white family. At first, it was hard having a new family, but their love was evident from the beginning. They showered me in love, saved me from a future of pain and torture. To this day, I am their child. I am still loved. I'd take the beatings all over again if it meant my new parents would come into my life and save me. There is always sunshine after the storm. Some of our biggest blessings come after the most hurtful situations."

I thought about what John said. Was it true? Would I really get a blessing? Faith once told me that God blesses His children, but I never felt like I was His child. Would He bless me too? Maybe He already did. I turned to John and smiled. "You are my blessing, John," I told him. "Thank you for the dress and the shoes. Thank you for coming into my life."

He grabbed my hand and squeezed it. "I love you and your sister very much."

I felt weak. "Nobody ever told me they loved me before, except Faith."

John smiled softly. "Well, know that I do. You girls are my blessing. Anything you need, I'm here for you. I will give you the same love that my adopted parents gave me. No child should be without that."

And I believed him.

I always heard stories about bad men. Abusive men. Cheating men. Angry men. Rarely did I ever hear stories about that one good black man. That strong man. That man who could hold a family down with one hand. That man was John. He did everything for my sister and me, and I just hoped I didn't find some way to ruin it.

In the summer, Faith went to South Carolina State University for an academic program that lasted two months. She called home every night and we'd talk about everything that happened in our days. She told me about a boy she had met named David. He was a junior and captain of his basketball team, and would be going to the university on a full scholarship. They had been hanging out, going to the movies, and having fun. He gave Faith her first kiss.

"How was it?" I asked, thrilled that she had finally gotten her first kiss.

"It was good. I felt alive and excited like when Momma buys me new dresses. I think he's the one. But enough about me, how has Momma been?"

I frowned. "She and John been having problems. She kicked him out of her bedroom and he now sleeps on the couch. I'm afraid that he's gonna leave."

"No, he ain't. You even said he told you he's only staying around for us."

"A man only gonna stay around for so long," I told her.

"Forget about their drama, how you been, Hope?"

I sighed. "I'm okay."

Truth was I was far from okay. I was depressed. My world was crashing all around me. It seems like Faith had been gone forever and I felt more alone than ever. Momma barely said a word to me, and if she did, it was only to ask how Faith was doing. John spent more and more time away from the house. I tried multiple things to get him to stay around more but Momma was too bothersome. I didn't blame him. If I had the chance, I'd stay away too.

But I was still alone and trapped. I didn't have anyone to talk to. Yes, John was great, but I couldn't open up to him the way I wanted to. Only Faith knew my heart's pain. But I couldn't lose John. I'd do anything I needed to do to make sure he stayed. I loved him. Maybe too much.

A loud crash coming from the living room snapped me from my trance. I heard Momma curse. "Faith, I'm gonna call you back." I hung up the phone before she could protest. John was now yelling, drowning out my momma's shouts. I put my ear up to my bedroom door and listened.

"You don't do nothing for me, John! I don't need you. You ain't nothing!" Momma screamed. I heard another loud crash. It sounded like a plate smashing into the wall.

"Stop throwing stuff, woman! And what do you mean I don't do anything for you? I pay half your bills and I love your kids more than you do." Something else slammed into the wall close to my door, making me jump back for a second.

"You love my kids more than me? Are you serious right now?"

"What have you ever done for Hope? You don't think it's wrong to spoil Faith and leave the other twin hungry for love?"

"Don't you question how I raise my kids. Them my kids. They ain't yours."

"They shouldn't be yours either."

I heard Momma gasp. "You can get out of my house if you don't like how I raise my kids!" she threatened.

"Naw, I'm gonna stay right here on this couch."

My heart leaped. I opened my bedroom door and walked into the living room, seeing broken dishes lying in piles on the floor. John was sitting on the couch and

Momma was standing over him with a plate in her hand. She looked at me and threw the plate at my head. Luckily, I ducked in enough time. Momma started to reach for another plate on the living room table but John stood up and pushed Momma away from it.

"Don't put your hands on me, John!" she screamed.

"Don't throw dishes at your kid! She didn't do anything to you!"

"Her presence is enough to get dishes thrown at her!"

John's fingers clenched into a fist and he started shaking. He lifted one finger and pointed to Momma, his eyes piercing into her. "If you ever put your hands on that girl while I'm around, I will beat you like you beat her, and you ain't gonna live to call the cops or kick me out. Think I'm playing?" He yanked her toward him. "I don't put my hands on women, but you ain't no real woman. If these kids can't fight, then I'll do it for them. Try me."

I watched Momma stumble back when he let her go. He stormed passed me into their bedroom and slammed the door. I turned around to Momma, who looked more like me than ever: cowering, afraid, defeated. It was hard to hide my grin. For once she knew how I felt.

Chapter 7

I didn't see John again until that next day. He was in the kitchen making breakfast. I had just showered and curled my hair and was ready to start my day. Momma said she needed to get away for a few days and had John pay for her to get a hotel in the city. I knew all she really wanted was just to be away from me. It was a relief to know that the cause of the tension was no longer in the house. I felt good about today. Nothing would bring me trouble.

I took a seat at the kitchen table and watched John cook the way I used to when he first moved in. He looked over at me and smiled. "Good morning, sleepyhead."

"Top of the mornin' to yer!" I said in a terrible Irish accent, causing his smile to widen. "What are we gonna do today?"

"Church?" he asked, catching me off-guard.

I choked on the orange juice I had picked up from the table and taken a sip of. *Church.* I had never gone to church. I had never thought it was a possibility. Did I want to go? No. I didn't. I never wanted to go to church. I was repelled by it. I was afraid of church. I thought that if I stepped inside, I'd burn. That's what Momma used to tell me when I was younger.

"No," I said kindly, but he didn't go for it.

"I thought you always wanted to go, since they never let you."

"Church ain't for me, ain't never been for me." I tried to hold back tears. I hadn't realized the topic of church was still such a fresh wound. I still hadn't dealt with how differently Faith and I had been treated. She was allowed to go to church and I wasn't. It still hurt and John sensed my anxieties.

"Hey," he said, turning away from the stove to look at me. "Church is for everyone."

"Not me. I ain't never been welcomed there and I don't ever plan on going."

He thought for a moment. "Do you believe in God?"

"Honestly? No," I told him, feeling frustrated that he was asking me about God. "I mean sometimes I do, when I need to pray to something, but then I remember He ain't never been there for me. If He wanted me, He would've called to me. Faith told me stories about how God worked in the old days, how He spoke to people. She said David would call on God, and He would save him from his enemies. God ain't never do that for me. So I don't do nothing for Him. I don't care about church or that Christian life. Momma said I was the devil. Devils don't care about church."

"Hope, don't let your momma define you. You are stronger than her. You can make your own decisions," he told me. "Take control of your life. If you wanted to go to church, you can walk right in and go. And God loves you. It wasn't Him that kept you from church, it was your momma and your grandmother. Don't take it out on God."

I felt it was God's fault too, but I didn't say anything. I was tired of hearing people try to convince me to change the opinions that were branded into my head from childhood. It's what I believed. It's what I knew and had accepted a long time ago. It would, no pun intended, take an act of God Himself to get me to change my mind.

Later that day, John and I sat out under the willow tree in the front yard. He pushed me on the tire swing as he told stories about the good times in his childhood. The sun began to set, casting a beautiful orange haze in the sky. John stopped pushing the swing, which caught me off-guard. I grounded my feet and turned to John, who was having a moment staring off into the sky.

He looked down at me and smiled. "God speaks to us through nature, we just don't listen. We've detached ourselves from nature, building houses to cage us in, roads to keep us from touching the earth, but God still does things for us to notice. Look." He pointed to the sky. "God gives us moments in each day to smile, thank, and acknowledge Him. When I see a sky that beautiful, I think . . . God is good. Go into a forest and just sit there and listen. You wouldn't be able to come back and tell me that you didn't feel the best sense of peace. The wind, do you ever listen to it?"

I smiled. I had listened to it. I felt that I could almost hear someone talking to me.

"One day, sit outside for hours and listen to it, listen until you hear it. It's God telling you something. He's always trying to tell us something. We've just forgotten how to listen." He walked around to face me. "Close your eyes." I did as he said. "Breath in and out, slowly. Keep your feet planted on the ground, spread our arms, let all of your worries go, and feel the earth's energy surge through you. Now listen to it, listen to what it has to tell you. Let God speak to you."

I tried to focus, but John was so close and so passionate, I couldn't focus on anything but his soft voice. I opened my eyes. He was standing there with his arms spread out, eyes closed, face tilted up, listening to something I couldn't and wouldn't hear. I began to admire his beauty. He was only thirty years old, five years younger than Momma, but his eyes held the wisdom of a man twice his age. Momma was stupid to put this man down. If he'd been mine, I'd have cherished the ground he walked on. I would have done anything to please him. Momma didn't deserve him. He didn't deserve the unhappiness she caused him. *Maybe I could make him happy. If I did, maybe he'd stay longer. Maybe he'd never leave.*

I stood up slowly, staring at his parted lips. I wanted to kiss those lips the way Momma couldn't. Make him feel the way Momma refused to make him feel. We were the same. He understood me and I understood him.

I quickly pressed my lips against his and stepped back, waiting for him to rage. John's forehead furrowed as he opened his eyes and found mine. I knew what he'd say, that I shouldn't have kissed him, but I didn't want to hear it.

"John, please don't be mad at me. I just love you so much and I couldn't contain it."

He sighed. "Hope, I love you too, both you and your sister, but you don't kiss me. I'm a grown man. You should kiss boys your age."

"Them boys ain't nothing but stupid," I told him. "What's wrong with me?"

"Your age."

"Back in the day, men your age married young women like me, even younger. I'm sixteen. In two years I'll be legal, and then we can run off together and leave Momma behind and be happy. Just you and me," I told him, smiling as I said every word, smiling like it would work.

"Hope, you're still a child and I love your momma."

"How can you love her? She don't even love you!" I yelled. I clenched my fist, trying to contain the anger I felt. How could he reject me? He said that he loved me and I had always been in love with him, I just didn't know it until that moment. "No man ever loved me like you love me, John."

"You're confusing the love of a father with the love of some little boy."

"You ain't my daddy. You can't love me like a father loves his daughter. Don't lie to me, John. You want me too." I walked up to him, rubbing my hands down his stomach. He gently moved them away. "John, let me make you feel good, like you make me feel. Let me touch you." I reached for his manhood, but he pushed my hands away, backing up.

"Hope, stop."

"No, John. Please, love me."

"No, Hope, stop!"

I stopped advancing toward him. My heart felt crushed into a million pieces. "You don't love me?"

He sighed, rubbing his eyes in frustration. "You know I love you, Hope, but—"

"Then prove it to me. Momma ain't gotta know. She ain't never gotta know."

He shook his head. "No."

I nodded once and ran away. I heard him shouting for me but I didn't care. I ran back into the house and into my room. I locked my door and threw myself on my bed and cried. I didn't care about putting a pillow over my head to drown out the noise. I wanted to world to hear my pain. Rejection is cruel. I felt it from Momma, Grandma, and now John. I no longer wanted to live if love was not an option.

John knocked on my door a few times that evening, but I ignored him. I ignored my sister's phone call. I ignored the world.

John had to love me. We were so close to each other, so open. He told me his secrets, ones no one else knew. We were closer than Momma and him. Even closer than Faith and me. I just knew I wasn't being delusional.

Somewhere along the night, I decided that I wasn't
going to give up. I knew John had to have wanted me too.
I went into Momma's bedroom where John slept while
she was gone and crawled in next to him. He groaned
in his sleep but kept snoring. I felt under the covers and
placed my hand on his bare chest and journeyed down
south. I had never touched a man like that before, but I'd
have done anything for John.

"Juanita . . ." he mumbled in his sleep, turning toward
me. I scooted closer, kissing his neck, rubbing on him,
feeling him get excited under my touch. "Juanita . . ." He
reached for me, touching my breast, pulling me closer. I
let out a moan and his eyes snapped open. "Hope!"

"Shh," I said, scooting closer before he could protest.
"Please. Just let it happen." I started kissing his tensed
neck, pulling his arms around me, pushing my hips to his.
He groaned deeply, trying to resist the temptation, but
I knew I'd won by the way his manhood responded. He
finally gave in and began to undress me. I was beautiful
girl; he wouldn't have been able to resist for long.

I let him remove my clothes, feeling victorious.

"This will be our secret," I whispered.

That next day, my body hurt in strange places, but it
was a good kind of pain. I felt like a woman. I walked
taller and with a purpose. My smile was wider. I felt loved
and for the first time. When I had woken up, John was
already out of the bed. I was slightly hesitant about what
would happen between us after that night.

I walked out of the room in my pajamas and saw John
in the kitchen, making breakfast like usual. I shrugged.
Maybe not much had changed. I took a seat at the kitchen
table and waited for him to speak. He acted as if I weren't
there. I smirked, stood up, and wrapped my arms around
him from the back. "You're not talking to me?"

He tensed but didn't move. "Good morning."

"Great morning . . . and night."

He sighed and turned to me. "Hope, what we did last night—"

"Was amazing. It was the best gift of love you could give me."

"I don't see it that way." John looked torn and weary . I could see the darkness forming under his eyes.

"Then change how you see it. What we did wasn't wrong. What Momma don't know won't hurt and ain't no point in regretting what you can't change. Might as well embrace it."

"It's not going to happen again," he said, and yet he didn't move away from my touch. "Crushes from little girls should be innocent."

"I ain't innocent and I ain't every girl. Besides"—I laughed—"you just made me a woman."

He finally pushed my hands away from him and turned to face me. His face was serious. "Hope, it's not going to happen again." His words sounded final.

Of course I snuck back into his room that night and let him have his way with me again. We kept at it until Momma returned a few days later. I liked what John and I did. It was an outlet, a way to forget about the pain inside even if it was only temporarily. I didn't like how tormented John felt because of his actions. It was eating him alive. He wasn't at peace with himself. He walked around the house heavily. He sighed often or cursed under his breath. I imagined he was shunning himself over and over again. I was just glad that he had a conscious. I sure didn't.

As much as Momma had hurt me, I couldn't have cared less about hurting her. Tit for tat. Was I wrong for feeling that way? At the time I didn't care. I was taking charge of my own life, doing what I wanted to do. I only saw what I wanted, and would have it at whatever expense. Besides, it was our secret. What Momma didn't know wouldn't hurt.

Momma made it be known that she was back. She stumped into the house, cursing me out for not cleaning, even though the house was spotless. She cursed John for no reason at all. I wanted to tell her about my love affair with her man, just to throw it in her face. I wanted her to hurt like she hurt me. And yet, when I had the opportunity, I couldn't do it.

"Hope!" Momma screamed from the kitchen, making me jump. I quickly walked into the kitchen thinking John had told her. Thinking she'd found out. She looked at me like I was a piece of trash and then handed me the phone. "It's your sister."

I sighed in relief.

I kept the secret even from my own twin. I couldn't break her heart or ruin her impression of John. He was a good man, the best man, and she loved him too. I was glad that it wasn't in the same way. I was sick of her taking everything I wanted.

At the end of the summer, Faith came home. She found me in the bathroom, throwing up, and sat beside me, brushing my hair back the way she used to when we were younger. She handed me some tissue and sighed.

"This ain't the welcome I thought I'd get," she said. I looked up at her from the toilet; there was a happy glow in her eyes. I sat up and smiled. I didn't realize how much I missed her until then. "I got a lot to tell you, girl!"

Faith and I went outside for a walk, heading toward the white church the way we did when we were twelve. She began telling me all about her time at the university and how she met new friends, went to some college parties, and fell in love. She seemed more at ease, more confident in her walk and her womanhood. She even dressed differently. When I asked her about it, she said, "This is how they dress in the city."

"Since when did you care about that?" I asked.

"Since I decided that I wanna go to that school." She glanced off, focusing on the cornfield while twisting her long hair with her fingers. There was something that she wanted to tell me. I could see the anxiousness in her eyes. "David called me as soon as I got home, saying he missed me already." Faith shook her head and laughed quietly. "Hope, I want to tell you something."

I was instantly excited. "Girl, tell me!"

Faith nodded and led me over to an opening in the cornfield where we sat. "I lost my virginity!" she exclaimed with wide, mesmerized eyes.

I almost choked. "You did?" I asked. "When?"

"Last night before I headed back home. David said we won't be able to see each other for a long time and that we needed to do it because it sealed our commitment to each other."

I almost laughed. "And you believe that crap?"

"He said he loves me," Faith spat.

I actually laughed out loud. "Faith, he don't love you. He only wanted what's between your legs. You're stupid!"

She stood up, obviously angry. "You're wrong, he does love me, but you wouldn't know what love is since you never had it!"

It was a smack in my face. Faith had never said anything like that to me. How could my own sister say that to me after seeing everything I'd gone through? I wanted to cry, but I wouldn't give her the satisfaction of knowing she'd won. I stood up too, facing her anger with my own.

"He don't love you, Faith. He'd say anything to get in your pants, and you was just dumb enough to believe him. Besides, I thought you read your Bible, little miss perfect. What God got to say about what you did?" I bellowed.

Faith gasped in surprise. "Don't throw the Bible in my face!"

"You've been throwing God in my face since the day Grandma took you to church without me!" I screamed. "You ain't so perfect now, huh? I wonder what Momma would think if she found out her precious angel ain't a virgin anymore!"

Faith grabbed a hold of my arm. "If you tell Momma, I'm gonna—"

"What are you gonna do, Faith? Tell God?" I laughed.

"You've always been jealous of me, waiting for me to mess up so that you could run and tell Momma I wasn't perfect. It wasn't my fault what happened to you, Hope."

"You didn't have to wear those dresses!" I told her. "You could've told Momma you didn't want to go to church!"

"I was a kid, Hope! Stop blaming me. I didn't understand it like I do now."

I didn't hear a word she said. I was too fueled to have any empathy. It was time for the truth to come out about everything. I was done keeping secrets, done keeping my mouth shut. Done living a life not fit for me.

"Nobody asked me how I felt! Nobody asked me if I was okay! You look down on me for not being a Christian, but you don't understand why I ain't one! I forced myself to hate church so I couldn't care less whenever you went without me. But deep down, I didn't hate church, because I still sat by that tree, listening to church songs and imagining a momma who loves me, a God that loves me! To have a sister who wasn't better than me at everything. To be given a fair shot to prove that I was a good girl! But now it's too late. I don't care about being good. I don't care about you and your perfection, I don't care about God, and I don't care about a loving mother. I don't care!"

"This argument started because you're jealous that I lost my virginity and you haven't because nobody wants you. Don't try to bring up the past now! Just accept the facts."

I laughed. "Do you want to know a fact, Faith? I lost my virginity two weeks ago. And you wanna know something else? He loves me, unlike that David boy. So what do I have to be jealous about?"

"You're lying."

"Oh yeah? Then why don't you go ask John."

Faith froze, avoiding eye contact. "How does John know about it? Did he catch you being nasty?"

"No, he knows because I was sleeping with *him* . . . in Momma's bed."

Faith reached out and smacked me, catching me off-guard. I held on to my cheek, fuming.

"You're lying."

"At first he felt bad, he didn't want to betray Momma, but I'd climb into Momma's bed anyway and he couldn't resist."

"Shut up, Hope!" Faith started to plug her ears. Tears were pouring down her face. She didn't want to believe it because she wouldn't be able to handle it.

"At first it hurt when he started making love to me, but after a while the pain started to feel good and I wanted it." At this point, I was in her ear and she pushed me away.

"Shut up!"

"I screamed for him to go deeper and he did," I taunted, knowing my every word was getting underneath my twin's skin.

"Shut up!"

"'Oh yes! Oh, John!'" I moaned, knowing each and every word was a punch to her face. I stopped abruptly, waiting for her to move her hands from her ears. When she did, I continued. "I love him. He loves me. You can be upset if you want but you will accept it. And if you tell Momma, I'm cutting you off."

I walked away, leaving her crying in the cornfield.

I felt victorious. The devil himself would've been proud.

Chapter 8

Faith stopped talking to me. She even started to act differently toward him, making sure she kept her distance. I had tried multiple times to start conversations with her, to make her laugh, but nothing worked. It was as if I became nothing to her, as if her opinions of me now mirrored Momma's. The only thing I could do was wait it out and hope Faith would come around.

After Momma had come home from her hotel, John ended our little relationship. It hurt, but I understood why. He loved my momma even though she didn't love anyone but Faith and herself. I was too distracted anyway to cry over John. Strange things were happening to my body.

I started to get sick a lot. Momma couldn't figure out why, but she kept me home from school until the sickness passed. I started to get bloated, irritated, exhausted; my nipples started to get sore, and I didn't want to eat anything. I walked into the kitchen one day when Momma was making eggs. The smell sent me flying over to the trashcan to throw up. Momma turned me toward her and started examining me. The first thing she did was feel on my stomach.

"You've been getting sick lately. You been having sex?"

"No, Momma."

"Don't lie to me," she said. "I been watching all your symptoms. I ain't stupid, Hope."

Momma walked over to the drawer in the kitchen she usually keeps random things in and pulled out a box. She then marched over to me, grabbed my arm, and dragged me into the bathroom. She shoved a pregnancy test into my hands while telling me she had bought one a week ago, but was waiting to see if I'd improve before she jumped to conclusions. She unbuckled my jeans and stood back. When I didn't move quick enough, she started yelling.

"Pee on the dang stick!"

My heart started racing. I slowly pulled my pants down and sat on the toilet. Momma crossed her arms and tapped her foot impatiently.

"Pee on the stick. Don't make me tell you again," she said.

I did as she said. Once I was done, she snatched the test and set it on the sink. She picked up the box and read the directions. I zoned out, thinking about the possibility of being pregnant. What would John say? Would he be happy? Would he leave my momma and get us a nice apartment in the city and we'd live happily ever after? I hoped.

Momma smacked me off of the toilet, bringing me back to reality. She had the test in her shaking hand. I stood up, pulling up my pants, trying to escape before she could hit me again. I ran passed her into the living room where John and Faith sat, watching TV. Momma came chasing after me. She grabbed a hold of my hair and yanked me back until I fell on the floor.

"She's pregnant!" Momma cried. "I knew it would be your fast butt! That's why I told you that you couldn't date until you were eighteen. I knew exactly what you'd turn out to be, nasty and disgusting! I wish I never had you!"

Faith ran to my side, helping me to my feet. As soon as she did, she seemed to regret it and went to stand next to our fuming mother. I looked at John, who sat frozen, staring at the pregnancy test in Momma's shaking hand.

"Which one of these little nappy-headed boys did you sleep with? Huh?" Momma smacked me from behind, causing John to stand up. "Answer me!"

I started crying. Too much had happened in such a short time, I wasn't even able to understand the extremities of my situation. I was sixteen and pregnant . . . by my momma's boyfriend. How could I tell her? How could I even raise a baby? I ran straight for John. He always knew what to do, but Momma snatched me back.

"Where you think you going? Huh? Answer the question! Who did your nasty butt lay up with?"

I would've loved to see the hurt in my mother's eyes when I told her the baby was her man's, but I decided not to tell her, and only for John's sake. I didn't want him to get in trouble for having sex with a minor. I'd run away before I told her.

Faith started crying hysterically. "I can't lie. God said we shouldn't lie. I can't do it!" Faith turned to Momma.

"No," I said, already knowing what she was going to say. "No, Faith! Please don't tell her!"

Faith ignored me, turning to Momma. I looked back at John, who sat down on the couch with his face buried in his hands.

"It's John's baby!" Faith pointed at John accusingly. "She told me she did it to John while you were gone. It's his baby!"

Momma's head slowly turned to John and then to me. Her hands clenched at her sides as she slowly inhaled. The pain was evident. And somehow, it made me feel good. I was expecting to feel remorse, pain, regret, but I felt nothing but joy in finally seeing Momma break the way I broke day after day. I thought back to everything she'd ever done to me, every beating, every negative comment, and it added fuel to my fire.

"Yeah, I did it, Momma. I slept with your man. I gave him what you couldn't."

Momma shook her head as tears dripped to the floor. "You're sick. You're crazy. How could you do that to me, your mother?"

How could I? I did it because John was the only person who loved me the right way. He didn't judge me, mistreat me, misuse me, throw things in my face, or hurt me. He only loved me, and yes, I may have confused my own feelings because I had never had a man love me, but it was love. Momma was the reason he came, but I was the reason he stayed. He told me he loved me. He said he'd never leave. Maybe I took it the wrong way. Maybe he was only trying to be the father I never had. At the end of the day, we did what we did and, at the time, I didn't regret a second.

We were going to have a baby. We were going to be a family. My life finally had meaning. I didn't need my momma or my sister anymore. All I needed was John. And in that moment of clarity, I grew strong before my momma.

"No, you're sick. It's all your fault, Momma!" She tried to protest, but I didn't let her speak. "I'm tired! I've been tired since I was a kid. You ain't never loved me. What have you ever done for me? Huh?"

"I loved you the best I could," Momma said, seemingly genuine.

"Ha!" I laughed. "You only loved Faith. But that's neither here nor there. Fact is, I'm pregnant with John's baby, and there ain't nothing you can do about it. I'm happy, Momma. Don't you see? I'm happy! Me and John are gonna get us a nice house and raise our baby."

Momma laughed through her tears. "You more stupid than you look. You think my man gonna run off with a kid and start a family? He already got a family, right here. Me and Faith. Go ahead, ask him where he gonna stay."

I turned around to John, who had stood up, sadly staring at both of us; but a decision was clear on his face.

"Go on, ask him." Momma's hands were still clenched at her sides.

"John." I walked up to him, holding my stomach, smiling. "We gonna have a baby. We can start a family, a real one."

"Ask him the question!" Momma shouted.

I swallowed hard. "John? You gonna choose me or Momma?"

John looked up to Momma; he wouldn't meet my eyes.

"John?" I asked, trying to turn his head toward me, but he kept his eyes on Momma. I heard her laugh behind me.

"Go ahead, John, you ain't stupid. Tell her that you staying right here where you belong. It probably ain't your baby anyway. She been fast since the day she was born. I'm sure she threw herself at you like the whore she is. Caught you when you were all weak and lonely."

"John?" I asked again, ignoring Momma. "Tell her. Tell her that the reason you stayed was because of me. Tell her it's the reason you gonna leave, too."

John finally looked down at me and shook his head. "Hope, I'm not leaving your mother. I'm sorry," he finally said.

I heard Momma laugh again.

"But, what about your baby?" I asked in desperation.

John squeezed his eyes shut as if in pain.

"Oh, he ain't gotta worry about that!" Momma said, yanking me away from John. "'Cause ain't gonna be no baby. You stupid little wench. You really think I was gonna let you get away with sleeping with my man and have his baby? Heck naw!" She slammed me to the ground. "'Cause I'm gonna beat that baby out of you!"

"No!" I cried, shielding myself from her attack. "John, please!"

Momma kicked me in my stomach repeatedly until the pain faded into numbness. She was too strong for me to fight back. She kept hitting me over and over again, while John and Faith just stood there in a catatonic daze.

Momma grabbed my hair and dragged me out on the front porch and kicked me down the stairs. I landed in dirt, instinctively grabbing my stomach. "No!" I cried out. "Why?"

Momma spat at me. "You ain't no child of mine. You the devil. That's why you ain't never go to church, because the devil can't step foot in it. I ain't even know I was having twins until you almost killed your sister in the womb. I had to get a C-section because your hands was closed around your sister's neck, causing her stress. The doctor laughed and said you was gonna be my problem child. He ain't never lied. But you ain't my daughter; you the devil child that was born along with my baby, Faith. You ain't welcomed back in this house. You won't be remembered. And since you so grown, go be grown on your own."

"Faith," I cried, watching her join Momma on the porch. I reached for my sister with eyes pleading for her to forgive me, to help me, but she just stood there, aloof and without compassion. My twin.

"She ain't your sister no more," Momma said, looking down at me in disgust. "She ain't nothing to you." Momma started coming toward me and I stood up, quickly backing away while holding out a hand to stop her. Every bone in my body ached. "Get out of here!" she spat.

"John!" I screamed for him, my throat burned from yelling and crying so hard. John said he loved me. He couldn't do this to me. "John!"

"Ain't no use screaming for him, he made his decision," Momma shouted. "Now get! Do I gotta beat you again?"

"I ain't leaving without John or Faith!" I proclaimed, which earned me a laugh from Momma.

"You gonna be standing out here until you die 'cause ain't nobody in this house stupid enough to side with a demon." Momma grabbed Faith's arm and headed back in the house.

I stood outside, waiting for someone to come back out, to forgive me, to let me back in, but nobody did. John betrayed me. He picked an old, crazy woman over his own baby. But I guessed the devil came in many disguises. I felt disgusted with myself, ashamed. I lost everything when the only thing I was trying to gain was love. I had nothing anymore. No momma, no sister, and no John. And so I ran. I ran until I couldn't run, and then I walked until I couldn't do anything but crawl. And somewhere along the way, I started to bleed between my legs. I don't know how long I crawled, but things started to darken even though the sun still shined. My throat started to constrict, the ground began rolling beneath me, and I was sucked into a deep wave, never quite able to come up for air.

Chapter 9

My body felt heavy, sedated. I tried to move my arms, but could barely manage the slightest movement. I inhaled, cracking my eyes open and quickly shutting them again once the bright white light dared to intrude. My body felt foreign to me. I tried wiggling my feet, and once that was a success, I began stretching out my legs. Eventually, my arms came back to life, and I slowly lifted a hand to wipe my eyes as I tried to adjust to the white light above.

I heard a door open and close, and then a hand softly pressed against my shoulder. "Please rest, honey, let the drugs wear off."

I turned to meet the voice. I could barely make out her face through all the sleep in my eyes. But her smile was big and reassuring. "Where am I?" I croaked.

"You're in the hospital, sweetie. You've been here two days."

"Why?"

"You were found unconscious and badly beaten on the side of the road. The doctors suspect you'd been lying out there for at least twenty-four hours. You were extremely dehydrated and in shock . . . and there's one more thing." I could now make out her face perfectly. She was a pretty white lady, mid-thirties, with sparkling gray eyes, brown hair, and a friendly smile. She was genuine and I liked her from the start. "You had a miscarriage."

My heart sank deep into my stomach. I gasped for air, grabbing at the white sheets at my side. My baby . . . John's baby . . .

Momma said she'd beat it out of me, and she didn't lie.

I felt the tears begin to threaten my resolve. "Okay," was all I managed to say.

"I'm so sorry, sweetie," she said, rubbing my shoulder. "I need to ask you some very important questions. It's procedure."

I nodded, not able to say much. All I could do was try to keep the pain inside. I'd save the misery for another day.

"How old are you?"

"Sixteen."

She removed her hand from my shoulder and began jotting down notes on a pad I'd just now realized occupied her other hand.

"Name?"

"Hope Williams."

"Where do you live?"

I blinked in response, caught off-guard. She eyed me patiently and I watched as her happy eyes darkened as she understood my unspoken words. She chose her next words carefully.

"How long have you been homeless?"

"Not long. My momma kicked me out and then I started walking and passed out." I looked around the hospital room. "And now I'm here."

The nurse's eyes never left mine. "Was it your mother who beat you?"

"No," I lied; it was instinct. Even when Momma hated me, I still protected her. I knew they'd probably put her in jail, charge her for murder, but she was still my momma. And somewhere in my heart, in some small corner, I loved her. I loved her enough to spare her the conviction she rightly deserved. I also had enough love for her so that if one day she ever decided to love me, there'd be some in return.

"Then who beat you? Do you understand that the police are going to come in here and question you? A serious crime was committed against you. You came in bruised, beaten, and bloody. Whoever hurt you made you lose your baby. That's murder!"

And the tears came, like a flood splashing down my face. "My baby . . ." I wasn't even given the chance to bask in the thought of a baby. I wasn't given the opportunity to smile and be happy or to regret it. I didn't get the chance to rub my stomach and smile, to talk to my baby, to think of names, to wonder if it was a boy or a girl. I didn't get the chance to make a promise to myself to be better to my baby than my mother was to me.

I finally had something to call my own. The best gift in the world. The one that would replace all the gifts I never got on my birthday or holidays. I lost my chance to be happy, to be loved.

"Who did this to you?" the nurse asked again.

I could've told her the truth. In fact, a big part of me wanted to make Momma pay for everything she ever did to me. A part of me wanted revenge on John, for denying me and my baby. A part of me wanted Faith to lose everything she loved, so that she could see how I felt. But even though Faith rejected me, I loved her too much to hurt her more than I already had. She was another reason I said nothing.

"I don't know who did it. It was a group of people." I looked the nurse right in her eyes and didn't blink. I could tell she believed me because she saddened and backed away. It was the best lie I ever told.

As the nurse had promised, the police officer visited me, questioning everything about me: who I was; where I lived; if I had any relatives who could get me; who attacked me; if I wanted to press charges and file a report. Everything. And of course I lied. I gave false names and false addresses.

He said that children services would be by later to pick me up because I was being discharged from the hospital. But by the time they came to get me, I was already gone.

For three nights, I slept on a park bench in the city. Freezing and shivering in my sleep. Jumping awake at the slightest noise knowing nothing could be safe about the city. I wasn't trying to get raped or killed. Multiple times I had thought about praying to God, wondering if He would actually hear the cries of His sinners. Faith had told me once that God turns a deaf ear to the wicked. So I didn't bother praying.

I constantly replayed in my head the image of Momma's shocked face when I told her I was pregnant by John. I always skipped over the part where I got beat, and losing my baby. Something about seeing Momma's pain made me sleep better on cold nights. Maybe it was because I liked knowing that I wasn't the only one suffering. I hoped then that she cried just thinking about it. I hoped she kicked John out so that he ended up with nothing, just like me. I thought he was a good man, and maybe he was, but one bad decision can ruin a person's image. I could've said the same for myself.

That next day, I was in need of a shower. I was still bleeding from after having the miscarriage; I had terrible cramps and found no relief. I didn't have any money and I needed a new pair of clothes and toiletries before I bled through my clothes. A corner store sat a few blocks down the street. My shirt was big enough to hide a few things and I decided to take my chances stealing the things I needed.

I walked into the store and paid attention to the fact that there were no security cameras or mirrors that would reflect what I was doing. The man at the register was an Arabic man who wasn't paying attention to me. He spoke loudly into his phone, turned toward shelves of cigarette cases. I grabbed a box of tampons and stuffed it under my shirt. I walked to the other aisle and grabbed some soap, toothpaste, and aspirin. I stuffed them under my breasts inside of my bra and was thankful for big boobs and a baggy shirt. I turned around and quickly left the store before the man even registered my presence.

I found the nearest restaurant and locked myself in the bathroom. I washed out my underwear, cleaned my body, freshened up, and left. I went to the cashier and asked for a cup of water. When she gave me the water, I swallowed three aspirin and sat down. The food smelled so good, I felt sick. I hadn't eaten in a few days. I walked back up to the counter and waited for the girl to come back to her register.

"Welcome to Burger Queen. What can I get for you?"

"Um, can I get a free sandwich?" I said barely above a whisper. I was embarrassed to be asking for free food.

"No, you have to pay for it. Only water is free," she told me kindly.

"But I ain't got no money and I ain't ate in a few days."

She looked concerned. "I'm sorry to hear that, but it's company policy."

"Can I talk to your manager?"

"He's not in today. I'm sorry."

"He ain't gonna know you gave me a sandwich," I said, hoping I could convince her, but she barely blinked.

"I can't," she said and hesitated before walking away. "I'm sorry."

I left the store feeling defeated. I was on the verge of breaking down. I was sixteen with nowhere to go, I lost my baby, and I hadn't eaten in days. I needed a miracle. Faith once told me that God knows what we need before we even know it ourselves. *If that's true, God must be like Momma, 'cause He never gave me anything I needed.*

I sat at a bench, watching a black car pull up in front of me. A woman got out of the driver's side and walked around to the passenger side and began helping an old lady out of the car. My eyes locked on the woman as she stood, straightening her back, taking a step forward with the cane in her hand. Maybe it was her godly appearance that attracted me to her. She was an old church woman, black and big and dressed to a tee in her church clothes. Her big purple hat matched perfectly with her suit. Dark sunglasses shaded her face, making it impossible to see her expression. She walked with a black cane and had the younger woman, maybe in her mid-forties, escort her inside a building. I was drawn to the woman like a moth to a flame. I didn't realize my feet had a mind of their own until they began guiding me to where the two women stood.

"Excuse me," I said, watching the younger woman turn around to me. I didn't know what I was going to say; I just felt the urge to be in the old lady's presence.

"Can I help you?" The younger of the two smiled.

"Who is it, Norma?" the old lady said with a deep country drawl that was melodic. She turned in my direction, looking at me, but her face still seemed to question me. "Who is it?"

"A girl." Norma frowned. Even when she frowned she was pretty. She reminded me of Faith, beautiful and light skinned, except Norma was aged by stress and maybe something else I couldn't put my finger on. Now that I saw her up close, I realized she couldn't have been older than forty. "Child, you look lost. Are you okay?"

"No." I didn't mean to tell the truth, but something about the old lady's presence made me want to.

She took a step toward me, seeming to not see me, and reached out her hand, feeling her way to my own. Once she had my hand, she squeezed. "Child, you got all your feet? All your teeth? All your toes and a working brain?" she asked.

"Yes."

"Then you're okay. As long as you ain't dying, you're okay," she said.

"I been sleeping on a park bench for days and I ain't had a good meal in about two. Am I still okay?"

She smiled and took off her glasses. Her unfocused eyes were gray and shadowed. "I'm blind. Am I okay?" She laughed out loud, sharing a joke with only herself. "Yes! And you are too. See, God always provides." She turned to where the other woman stood. "Norma, give this girl the money in my purse. God told me to carry all of this money on me today. I didn't understand why until now."

Norma quickly reached in the old woman's purse and handed me a large stack of money. I was speechless. Norma seemed to be as well.

"Take the money and get yourself a nice meal and a hotel." The old lady smiled again, oblivious to our shock. "You want the wisdom of an old lady? I've given you a seed, you plant it, water it, love it, and watch it grow. A fool spends all of his money in one day." She turned away from me and allowed Norma to escort her to the building.

"What is your name?" I asked her, feeling elated.

Norma stopped right before they entered the building and turned around to me. "Her name is May Baker," she said. "Pastor of Rising Faith Ministries."

I watched them go inside, hoping it wouldn't be the last time I saw her.

***

I did exactly what May Baker told me to do. I got myself a nice meal, making sure I didn't spend too much on food, and then I went around the corner to the cheapest motel and gave the man enough money to keep me sheltered for a week. Thankfully I had an ID at sixteen, but once the man saw my age, he began asking questions. I ended up tipping him thirty dollars to stop asking.

I sat down on my bed, counting the money while eating leftovers from my lunch. It was a total of $3,000. May Baker had given me $3,000! I wanted jump up and go shopping but remembered the bit of wisdom May Baker gave me, to plant my money and watch it grow. I didn't know what that meant, but I figured I'd start at the bank.

I sat with a personal banker for about an hour, going over opening a student checking account, establishing credit, putting my money into an account where the bank would match me a dollar for every dollar I would deposit. Thankfully they allowed me to open an account without a guardian.

After leaving the bank, I found the nearest thrift store and bought a week's worth of clothes for only twenty dollars. They weren't the best clothes but that didn't matter to me. I had something to wear. After that, I ordered Chinese food and watched TV in the motel until I fell asleep. I remember dreaming about my money turning into $6,000, and it kept doubling until I was a millionaire. It was a good dream. Too bad it wasn't real.

I woke up that next morning with the biggest urge to find May Baker, but I swallowed it. I didn't even know why I wanted to find her; I just knew that I did. Even when I swallowed the thought, I still felt it pressing at the corners of my mind.

Sitting around a motel thinking about all of the pain in my life was tiresome. I needed something to do. I needed to find a job. At sixteen, there were only a few places I could work and none of them seemed appealing. A thought occurred to me. Maybe May Baker needed someone to help her out. Norma looked tired and seemed to be getting too old to be escorting an old lady around, if that was what she did all day. Plus it was a way to pay May Baker back for her kindness.

I remembered Norma stating that she attended a church called Rising Faith. There had to be a way to contact her. I decided to spend that next day doing exactly that. I started off at the library a few miles away from the motel. I started searching her name and, when that failed, I tried searching for the church. Multiple Web sites mentioned the phenomenal church, noting its generosity and programs for the youth. Although interesting, I chose the actual Web site and found the address located at the bottom. I then put the address in the search engine and found the directions. It was just four miles away. I found the bus route and decided to go down to the church.

An hour later I stood in front of an old white stone church twice the size of the country church Faith went to. It was bordered with black metal gates that remained open for the public. The windows were made out of some type of stained glass I'd never seen before. They held images of Jesus and Mary and of angels that seemed to be looking right at me. All of it was too much. I was instantly stuck in once place, not wanting to move.

I hadn't really thought out my plan once I got to the church. I'd never stepped a single foot in a church and promised myself I never would. And here I was, looking for a blind old lady and questioning whether I should go inside. My stomach turned. I knew I didn't like churches but I hadn't realized churches placed such fear in my heart. I could barely breathe.

I stood there for about an hour, debating, before I decided to stand just outside of the church and wait until she either came or went. Eventually I got tired of standing and began sitting, watching the traffic pass by, wondering what lives those people lived, where they were off to, what mood they were in. By the time nine o'clock came, I realized I wasn't going to see the old lady and decided to leave.

I kept the same routine for three days that week. Sitting just outside of the church's gates, waiting to see the old lady come or go, but nothing. One that third day, around six o'clock in the evening, people began walking inside of the church, dressed in nice clothes, holding their Bibles.

I stood up from the ground when a woman stood in front of me with her hands on her hips. She cocked her head to the side. "Girl, I rode passed the church the other day and saw you sitting out here, and now I'm back for Bible Study and you're still sitting out here? Are you homeless or crazy?"

"I'm waiting for May Baker."

"Pastor Baker is old and can't move around like she used to. She only comes to church on Wednesdays and Sundays for Bible Study and service. Why don't you come inside? I'm sure she's already here. You might've missed her."

I hesitated. "Um, no, I'll wait outside."

She wrapped her blue shawl around her body. "Child, it's chilly outside. You gonna catch a cold if you keep standing out here like that. Come on inside."

I shook my head. "No, I'm not cold. I'll wait outside."

The woman looked me up and down, frowning. But she left me alone and went inside. I sank back onto the ground and pulled my arms inside of my shirt for more warmth and waited.

I hadn't realized I'd fallen asleep until a soft voice interrupted me. I opened my eyes to a dark evening and Norma standing over me. May Baker stood on the sidewalk, waiting.

"Girl, why are you outside of the church sleeping?"

I pushed my arms through my shirt and sat up. "I want to talk to May Baker."

Norma looked back at May and then focused her hard eyes on me. She helped me to my feet and took me over to where May stood.

"It's the homeless girl from the other day, Momma," Norma said, standing aside for me to be able to talk to May. I hadn't realized Norma was May's daughter.

May smiled sweetly. "God told me you'd be back," May said, confusing me. I didn't know that God talked to people. Faith said He used to talk to people back in the day. I guessed it wouldn't be any different now. "What is the problem, child?"

"I want to thank you for giving me that money and I want to repay you," I told her. "Maybe I can help you out through the week? I can come by your house and clean and cook, take you places. I can't drive, but I can learn, and I don't really know the city, but—"

"Hold on, baby," May Baker said softly. "Let me get this straight. So you're volunteering to help me out around the house to repay me for the money I gave you? Honey, that was Jesus' money, repay Him, not me."

I thought about it for a minute. "I can repay Him by helping you out. Faith used to tell me that God loves it when His people love each other like they love themselves."

"Who's Faith?" May asked.

"My twin." I really didn't want to talk about her, so I changed the subject. "Can I please help you?"

"Momma, the girl seems nice and we could use the help." Norma turned to me. "We need someone to help out around the house while I'm at work. You can come over in the mornings for a few hours." She grabbed a piece of paper and pen from her purse and began writing on it. "From nine to twelve, or for however long you want to stay and help. The address and phone number are on the paper."

I took the piece of paper from her with a smile. "Thank you!"

"No, honey, thank you," Norma said, and continued guiding May to the car. "We'll see you tomorrow?"

"Yes, ma'am!"

Chapter 10

That next day, I stood in front of a Victorian-style home. The land was spacious but dying. The grass had brown patches that stretched across the yard. The garden was unattended and messy. The paint on the house was beginning to chip, making the house look slightly haunted. I could imagine how beautiful the house once was, before May Baker was too old to keep it up.

Aside from the work that needed to be done, the house was still beautiful. It looked like a small castle, with a multifaceted structure. The roof pointed sharply to the sky at different locations, making the house look like it held four or five levels. The roof was black, as well as the shutters and front door. And just like Momma's house, this one had a beautiful weeping willow tree that sat in the front yard. I could see multiple trees swaying behind the house in the backyard.

I walked up on the porch, noticing the porch swing to my left and a few chairs with a table to my right. A glass of lemonade still sat on the table with ice floating. Someone had been sitting on the porch not too long ago.

Before I knocked on the door, Norma came rushing out of the house accompanied by two children, a boy and girl around seven years old. She looked up to me absentmindedly and managed a smile when she saw me. She guided the kids down the stairs and stopped to talk to me. Up close, I could see the exhaustion that slouched her shoulders.

"Momma's in the house taking a nap. I stop by every morning before work to check on her and make sure she's taken her medicine and eaten. I left details on the kitchen table. It'll tell you when she takes her medicine and which medicine she takes. Now she's already had her morning medicine and won't be due for more until noon. So every day before you leave, give her the medicine. It's very important. I'll be back around six tonight, so she'll be on her own after you leave, but she's capable of caring for herself. She just really needs help around the house, there is a lot of cleaning she can't do. I left my number on the table just in case you ever need to call me." She said everything in a rush, but I was sure I had gotten the gist of it. She smiled and turned toward her car, shouting to her kids to buckle their seat belts, and then she was gone.

I grabbed the lemonade off of the table, figuring May forgot it outside, and stepped into the house. The inside was nicer than what I thought. May had a spacious living room with a tan couch set and glass tables. A forty-two-inch flat-screen TV sat against the wall. The channel was broadcasting a sermon from Pastor T.D. Jakes. May sat upright on the couch and had dozed off. I took the opportunity to explore her house. I walked through the living room, taking in the fireplace and the decorated mantel. Pictures of Norma's kids sat atop it, along with porcelain elephants.

I walked into the kitchen, impressed by its size. A nice table sat in the middle of the room. A fruit basket was centered on the table and the note sat beside it. I placed the lemonade on the table and picked up an apple and bit into it. With the other hand, I went through the cabinets, memorizing where May kept her spices, food, and dishes. I opened her refrigerator, staring at all of the food. I picked up a carton of skim milk and quickly placed it back. "Nothing but a bunch of old people's food." I closed the door and headed into what looked like a nice dining area, with a larger, sturdy table, made of a beautiful dark wood. She had it decorated with nice flowered placemats, and dishware. Fresh flowers sat in the middle of the table and the sunlight from the window reflected off of the crystal chandeliers, painting diamonds on the walls.

I skipped past the bathroom and made my way back to the front of the house and walked upstairs, listening to the steps creak. The first room was locked. I continued past the bathroom and opened the third door, which led to a bedroom with flowered wallpaper, a full-sized white bed, and a brown dresser. I closed the door and headed to the last room.

And then I heard May downstairs coughing.

I left the last bedroom and went back downstairs to check on May, who was still sleeping. I was about to finish exploring the house but heard a knock at the front door. I opened the door, greeted by a boy around my age who was so light skinned his cheeks were pink. He looked shy and smiled at me sweetly.

"Is Pastor Baker here?"

I folded my arms, which was a defensive mechanism whenever I met new people. "She's taking a nap, who are you?"

"I'm Dante, I go to her church."

"Do you need something?"

He smiled again. "I come over every day to keep Pastor Baker company."

"Well, she's asleep and I'll be keeping her company today."

He frowned. "I come over to play checkers with her. It's her favorite game. Do you know how to play?"

"No."

"Well, she's going to want to play." He tried to step inside but I blocked him.

"I'll learn," I said and shut the door. I took a seat in the chair next to May and I, too, eventually dozed off.

I woke up to quiet voices. I stood up, stretched and then walked to the window and peeked out. I had the perfect view of May and Dante outside on the porch playing checkers. I jumped up and walked out on the porch as they were laughing. Dante was first to look up.

May smiled. "I didn't want to wake you up, honey. You seemed so peaceful."

"What time is it?" I asked, rubbing my eyes.

"It just turned eleven. Dante made some sandwiches in the kitchen if you're hungry. Can you bring me some more lemonade?" She picked up the glass from the table and handed it to me. I smiled and walked back into the house. As I poured her drink, I picked up the house phone and dialed home. I was beginning to miss Faith with each passing day and needed to hear her voice. I knew she probably hated me, and I didn't blame her for it. I hated myself.

The phone picked up on the third ring. "Hello?" Faith's voice was sweet to my ears.

"Faith." I didn't know what else to say. I slowly placed the lemonade back into the refrigerator as I thought.

"Hope?" she asked. "Why did you call here? You know Momma will flip out if she found out you called."

"Faith, I'm—" But before I could finish, Momma's voice shouted through the phone.

"Why are you calling my house? Your sister don't wanna talk to you. Don't call my house again!"

"But, Momma—" I started, but the phone hung up.

I quickly grabbed the glass of lemonade and took it to May before I could break down crying. I held it all in, taking a seat in the third chair beside May. She took a drink of her lemonade and set it down. She felt for her pieces to make her next move. I didn't understand how she could play checkers being blind. I looked at Dante, who eyed me curiously as if he knew something was wrong with me. I narrowed my eyes, showing my attitude. He looked back at the game shyly.

I studied him as he played, wondering who he was and where he came from. I didn't understand how a boy his age found playing checkers with an old, blind woman interesting, but I wasn't going to judge. He seemed slightly nerdish and innocent but he had a boyish beauty that would turn any girl's head. I wouldn't mind staring at his pretty face but that didn't mean I had to like him.

Twenty minutes later, Dante was gone and May was back inside, eating a sandwich so that she could take her medicine at twelve. She was quiet for the most part, probably waiting for me to speak, but I didn't. I was too wounded by the phone call to speak. May sensed it; I could tell by the way she sat staring into my direction as if she wanted to say something.

"You go to church, Hope?"

"No, ma'am."

"Why not?"

I shifted uncomfortably in my seat and changed the subject. "Does Norma live with you?"

"No." If May noticed the change of subject, she didn't mention in. "She lives with her two kids in an apartment on the other side of town."

"Are you married?"

"I'm widowed with two daughters. My husband used to be the preacher of Rising Faith Ministries but he died many years ago." A shadow of sadness shaded her eyes.

"I'm sorry."

She smiled, bringing joy back into the room. "He was a good man. I never thought I'd get married but God brought him into my life after many prayers."

"He never answers mine," I mumbled, but she heard me.

"God always answers our prayers. Sometimes the answer is 'wait' or 'no,' but He always answers."

I didn't like where the conversation was going and changed it again. "What all do you need done around the house?"

She thought for a moment. "Is the grass high? It ain't been cut in a week."

I stood up. "I'll cut it."

About thirty-five minutes later, I walked back into her house sweaty and tired. May stood in the kitchen, finally taking her medicine. I quickly grabbed the paper and scanned over it, making sure she was taking the right medicine. She smiled and waved me away.

"I've been taking care of myself my whole life, I can manage my pills. Please get me some water."

I grabbed her glass, washed it out, filled it with water, and handed it to her.

"Why are you homeless?" Her question caught me off-guard. I guess I had been expecting that she'd begin asking questions but did I really want to open up to her? Was I ready to tell someone my history when they already thought highly of me? I didn't want to ruin my newfound reputation.

"I ran away after my mom died."

She sighed. "The good thing about being blind is that all of your other senses are heightened. I can hear a lie a mile away. It's in the sound of your voice. My momma died when I was young. I know the pain and, child, you ain't got that pain. Don't lie in my house."

I was shocked and swallowed hard. I could feel the sweat on my forehead. "I don't want you to judge me."

She turned toward the sound of my voice. "Child, only God can judge. I won't judge you. Ever."

"Well . . . I got kicked out of my house."

"Why?"

"I don't wanna say."

"Child, if you plan on being in this house, I need to know your background."

I sighed. "Because I got pregnant."

May almost dropped her medicine. "How old are you?"

"Sixteen."

"And how far along are you?"

"I'm not." A thousand emotions surfaced, ranging from anger to dread. I suddenly felt claustrophobic and needed to escape. "She beat the baby out of me and then kicked me out."

May's medicine fell from her hands and at least twenty pills slid off of the table on to the ground. I quickly dropped to my knees, picking the medicine up. They all ranged in color and size. It was impossible to know which pills belonged where but I busied myself with trying to figure it out so that I wouldn't have to stare at May's shocked expression.

"Don't worry about the pills, child. Norma will sort them out when she gets here." Right after she said it, the grandfather clock came alive, singing. "It's twelve o'clock. You can leave. I'll have more for you to do tomorrow."

"Thank you," I said, almost too low, and left her house. I was thankful to have finally escaped, like I always did whenever faced with my problems.

I came back the next day just as Norma was leaving. Her kids waved at me as they passed me by on the walkway. She stopped and talked to me, and, by the indifferent look on her face, I could tell May hadn't told her about my miscarriage. It gave me some comfort.

"Thanks for helping out yesterday. I have a new list for you so that you'll know which medicine goes in her cases just in case another incident happens. She also has a list of things written she needs you to do." She smiled and followed her kids to the car.

She didn't lie when she said May had a big list of work for me. I had to look over the list a few times before it fully registered. I was happy about it because it would keep my mind busy. I started with going out back into her shed and getting a ladder. Spring was around the corner and May needed to get the leaves out of the gutter. She also wanted me to rake the old leaves left over on the ground from fall, organize her shed, and lay soil down in her garden so that we could plant flowers. I didn't understand what flowers did for a blind person but I guessed it was for others to enjoy when they came over.

I was good and sweaty by the time Dante came over. He scared the mess out of me as I was climbing down the ladder after cleaning the shutter.

He tried to hold in his amusement at my reaction to him scaring me. "What are you doing?"

"Cleaning the gutter." I folded my arms defensively. I really didn't know how to take to men, even the ones who barely looked eighteen.

"Need help?"

"Ain't you supposed to be playing chess?"

"It's checkers, and no. I don't always come to play checkers. Sometimes her medicine kicks in before I get here and she goes to sleep so I start helping out around the house. I saw that long list and I know you need help."

"No, I don't," I said with an attitude, hoping it'd make him go away. I had no desire to spend time near a boy, not after the heartbreak I'd suffered. "It keeps me busy." I started stuffing leaves into a trash bag, ignoring Dante's presence.

"It keeps you busy from what?"

I stood straight, facing him. "Can you leave me alone before I go off!"

He laughed, immune to my attitude, and walked away. I began shoving leaves into the trash bag with more speed than before. After I was done with the gutters, I worked on raking up the yard, which took me an hour. After I was done, I set the bags by the Dumpster and began working on the shed.

I lost track of time, but didn't care. It felt good doing things, staying busy. At some point, I started to hum the old Negro spiritual songs I used to sing whenever I sat outside during church service as a child. I hadn't sung those songs in years, and I never did understand why that church sang all of the old songs instead of the gospel songs of that time.

A knock on the shed made me jump. Norma stood in the doorway. Had I been in the shelter for that long?

"Momma said you'd been out here all day cleaning up the shed. She figured it would take you a week clean all of this up." She stepped inside, looking around at the organized shelves and tools that I hung on the walls. "It's after six. I'm making dinner, are you hungry?"

"Yes," I said.

"Well, come on inside." Norma smiled, shutting the door as she left.

I looked around the shed at all of the work I'd accomplished. It felt good doing something besides sitting in a house all day being yelled at for stupid reasons. I felt a sense of purpose truly begin to form. I knew I was meant to be here, helping May. In the process of helping her, I would also be helping myself.

I locked the shed up and headed back inside. I entered into the dining room, watching Norma's two kids do their homework and play around. The boy was the hyper one, running around the table multiple times until his mom yelled for him to sit down. The girl stayed quiet, working on her homework and looking up at me every now and then. Norma headed back to the kitchen.

"How old are you?" I asked her, taking a seat at the table.

"We're both seven," the girl answered.

My eyebrows rose. "Who's older?"

"We're twins," the boy answered, bouncing in his chair.

Twins. Like Faith and me. The boy reminded me of myself, hyper and happy, while the girl sat quietly and thoughtfully, like Faith. It almost brought tears to my eyes.

I turned to the boy. "Did you get presents on your birthday?"

His face lit up. "Momma got me a Spiderman toy and my cake was Spiderman!"

"Mine was a princess cake!" the girl said. I smiled at the equality, something I didn't know myself. It made me happy knowing other children didn't have to ask why their mommy didn't love them.

Norma returned with two plates and set each by the kids. She gathered their homework and put it in their book bags. May came into the dining area and Norma helped her to get seated. Norma went back into the kitchen and emerged with two more plates for May and me and then disappeared again. She returned with her own plate and sat across from May at the end of the table.

"Let's grace the food," she said and bowed her head. I watched as May and the kids bowed their heads, wondering what they were doing. "Dear Father, giver of all good, accept our praise and bless our food through Jesus Christ, our blessed Lord. Amen."

They all lifted their heads and began to eat. I frowned. "What was that?"

"What?" Norma asked.

"When you grace the food, why do you do that?"

"You've never graced your food?"

I shook my head. Momma never allowed any prayers at the dinner table. If Faith prayed over her food, it was done in silence.

It was May who answered my question. "We bless our food because we want to honor God in everyday activities, like eating. It also reminds us that God is the source of all we have. He gave us food and we thank and bless it so that we may be healthy."

I nodded my understanding and dug into my food. Norma cooked baked chicken marinated in balsamic vinaigrette, with greens and mashed potatoes. She was a good cook and I loved everything about her food. I felt full and healthy for the first time. It was the most normal meal I'd eaten in a while.

Norma had the next day off and didn't need me around the house, but I still came anyway. I liked being in that house, around May and Norma.

When I arrived, the kids were outside playing in the yard. May sat on the porch, drinking lemonade. I said hello and walked into the house. Norma was sitting at the table in the kitchen, talking on the phone. "Can we get set up on a repayment plan? What about a modification?" She sighed. "I just don't want to lose this house. My grandmother has been living here since she got married!" She sighed again. "Fine, just send the paperwork, thanks."

She turned around and saw me standing there and sighed again. "How much did you hear?"

"Not much," I lied.

"Well, whatever you heard, don't tell my grandmother. She doesn't know that we are underwater," Norma said.

"May is your grandma?" I was surprised. "I thought she was your mom."

"Because I call her Momma?" Norma smiled. "Momma May, that's what all her grandkids call her. She practically raised us. Momma is the kind of woman all women should aspire to be like. If it wasn't for her, me and my siblings would be reckless and into drugs like my real mother. You know how that is, don't you?"

"Huh?"

"Well, I assumed your mother was on drugs. No normal mother would allow their child to be homeless." She covered her mouth quickly. "Unless she passed away."

"No, she's alive."

"Come in here and sit down." I did as she said. "Why were you homeless then, Hope?"

Just as I was about to explain, Dante walked in with the twins clinging to him. He smiled at me and then directed his attention to Norma. "Your brats are destroying the yard," Dante said.

Norma stood up and guided her kids into the kitchen. "Time for homework!"

Dante took a seat where Norma had been sitting. "You goin' to church Sunday?"

I tensed. "No."

Dante frowned. "May thinks you are. She told me to come talk to you about the youth program we have."

"I . . . I ain't interested, but thanks." I went to stand but Dante grabbed my arm, gently coaxing me back in my seat.

"Why?"

"I don't go to church," I said in irritation. I was tired of people asking me.

"Why?"

"Can you stop asking me questions? I don't like you!" I screamed, standing up.

May stormed into the house, walking quicker than I'd ever seen her walk. She stopped a few feet away from me and pointed her cane. Her anger was evident. "Child, don't you come up in my house being nasty and fussin' at the boy because he asked you a question. That ain't nothing but the devil."

I flashed back to all the times Momma had called me the devil and sat down in the chair, defeated. Even an old church woman thought I was the devil.

"I ain't the devil," I mouthed back.

"I ain't say you was. I said being nasty and fussin' is the devil's doing and ain't got no place in my house! I'll wash your mouth out with soap! Tell the boy you're sorry," she demanded.

I looked at Dante, who sat smugly in his chair, smiling like he'd won a prize.

I frowned. "I'm sorry."

"I don't believe her!" he said quickly and smiled wider. I wanted to knock him out.

"I'm sorry for yelling and fussing at you, Dante," I said, exaggerating my pronunciation of each word.

He tried hard not to laugh, which lightened my mood up. I guessed it was somewhat funny. I never had much of a sense of humor.

"Come outside and talk to me, Hope," May said, turning back around and feeling her way back to the porch with her cane. I sighed and followed. May nestled in her chair, drinking a glass of water. I took a seat beside her and waited for her to speak. She didn't say anything for a while, and I started to wonder if she ever would.

"I've been thinking about what you told me about your mother beating you," she said. "Something similar happened to me when I was around your age. Back in 1948 I got my first job as a maid for the mayor and his wife. They were a beautiful couple and everyone admired them. The mayor had a certain charm that many women fell for. He slept around frequently. His wife knew about it, but being a woman in 1948 and having a strong opinion that objected her husband's was unheard of.

"I had been working there for about two months, everything was going good. The mayor was always away.

He was very much into his work. His wife stayed home and looked after the kids. During the winter, the mayor came around more. I noticed he had a drinking problem. There wasn't a day that went by that winter where I didn't see him drinking. I used to hear them argue upstairs. The next day I'd help his wife cover the bruises on her face with powder and makeup. I noticed how the mayor would watch me when I cleaned, it was how he watched the white women around town.

"In late January, his wife was ill in her pregnancy and was put on bed rest most of the day. I was working in the kitchen, cleaning the dishes when the mayor came behind me and began rubbing on me. I was afraid that he'd beat me if I didn't cooperate, beat me and then kick me out. I wouldn't have had a place to stay. So I let him touch me. He whispered in my ears, clasping my hips, telling me he loved my brown skin. Said he always had a fantasy for Negro women. And then he stumbled away.

"Same thing happened the second night. This time I was cleaning off the table when he came from behind and pushed me onto it. He . . . Well, I don't want to get too detailed. Somehow, memories like that never fade. I used to think that it was best to tuck them deep inside so that they wouldn't bother me from day to day. I was wrong. We have to let it out and give it to God. Well, he had his way with me that night. It happened over and over again for almost two months, and then I found out I was pregnant.

"I was young and stupid and ran straight to his wife, telling her everything that happened, hoping she'd believe me. I sat there with her through her tears, I thought she would've understood." May shook her head, disgusted. "But she could do to me what she couldn't do to the other women her husband slept with. She beat me, badly, and I lost the baby."

I listened intently as May continued.

"But it didn't stop him from doing what he did. She tried to kick me out but he wouldn't let it happen. He kept coming to me late at night, forcing himself on me, telling me he loved me . . . but he didn't. That man knew no love. I only ended up running away from that place. I took all of her jewelry and sold it and took a train to South Carolina, where nobody knew my name. The mayor and his wife found me. I was beaten so badly, they thought I was going to die. That was when I lost my sight. I didn't talk about it for a long time, even after I met my husband." She stopped, and smiled. I could tell it was a sweet memory she thought of. "He didn't care that I was blind and told me I was the most beautiful woman he'd ever seen, and that God told him to love me and to make me his wife.

"Hope, we gotta go through the bad to get to the good. We gotta suffer to know pleasure, to appreciate it. I could no longer see. This man took my innocence, his wife killed the baby inside of me, and together, they took my sight. Shouldn't I be angry? Shouldn't I jump up and scream at the world, hate people who are only trying to be nice to me? No. Because even then, God still had a plan. If I hadn't worked for the mayor, I wouldn't never ran away to South Carolina and met my husband. Life has a funny way of correcting itself and only God knows its ways. But God wills us to keep pushing, even when we're ready to give up. He keeps us strong, even when our own muscles fail us. You, Hope, you have a purpose. It might take awhile to realize what that purpose is, but it's there, waiting for you to claim it."

I was overwhelmed by her testimony, so similar to my own and yet so very different. I, too, held my deepest emotions inside, pushing them away so that I could make it through the day. I hadn't truly broken down over losing my baby, over losing John and Faith, because I was afraid that if I had broken down, I wouldn't get back up. I'd be too damaged to fix. I didn't want to know the extent of my pain; I didn't want to test it. I wanted to keep it buried deep inside, like May did. But even she said it's best to let it out.

I looked at the old lady beside me. She was blinded, beaten, and mistreated, but even after all of that, she was still able to smile. She got back up and lived a beautiful life. Maybe I could too. And she was right; we were a lot alike, in many ways. She had said she sensed a spirit similar to her own when she met me, and it dawned on me. I felt the same thing. It was why I was so intrigued by her in the first place.

"Come to church on Sunday. You really need to hear the message that I have," May said.

And just at the mention of church, it was as if everything she had said meant nothing now. I recoiled back into my shell, closing myself off because of an invitation to go to church. Too many memories surfaced of me being a little girl, crying every Sunday when Grandma took Faith to church, leaving me behind. Memories of me being hungry because Momma only had enough food to feed Faith before she went to church. Memories of praying that, one day, I'd be able to go to church like Faith. Thinking God hated me because I was a bad girl. Knowing Momma hated me . . . knowing she still did.

Nothing had really changed. I was still that sad little girl. "No, I . . . I don't want to go to church," I told her.

"I can hear the pain in your voice when you say it, child. Why?"

I hadn't realized I'd stopped breathing until I gasped for air. My hands were hurting from clutching my chair so hard. I felt like I was going to explode. All of the hurt was going to ooze out of me. I couldn't do it.

Just then, Dante came outside, saving me. I was never so thankful for his presence.

"May . . ." He stopped when he saw the pained expression on my face. "Is this a bad time?"

"No!" I almost shouted, standing up. I was relieved he came when he did because I didn't want to have that conversation with May. "Hey, Dante, wanna go for a walk? I need to get some exercise."

He frowned, not believing me, but I didn't care. "Okay," he finally said, and off we went before there could be any further discussion about church.

After we turned the first corner, I stopped and bent over. I tried to fight the tears that threatened to come, but they took over, making my body convulse as I silently cried. I felt Dante's hand on my shoulder, a friendly gesture I was sure, but I moved away, not wanting a man's touch. I forced myself to straighten and wiped my tears away and kept walking like nothing ever happened. Dante followed closely behind, giving me enough space to vent silently. For that I was grateful.

After about five minutes of walking, I slowed, finally in control of my own emotions. I didn't look at Dante but I knew he was still beside me. We were close to downtown; the houses had turned into buildings. The traffic was packed, cars zoomed by, blowing their horns and shouting at drivers ahead of them. People passed by on bikes and skateboards. A group of nuns smiled as they walked by.

"Do you know where we are?" I asked.

"Yeah," he said, matching my slowed pace. "Close to the church. It's around the corner. You wanna go check it out? I know how to get inside when it's closed."

"No. I don't do church. Ever," I said. "I wish people would stop asking me. You know what I want to do? Go to a party, be young, have fun, and get it crackin'!" I turned to him, inspired and excited. "Do you know how to get us in a club?"

"No," he said. "I don't do that stuff. I stay home and read my Bible. God said—"

I moaned and kept walking. "You sound like Faith."

"Who's Faith?"

"My sister. She always quotin' the Bible, too scared to go out and party. Square. And you remind me of Carlton from *Fresh Prince*." I looked at his clothes. He always wore dress pants pulled a little too high over his stomach and his shirt was always tucked in. He walked like he had something stuck up his behind.

"I like to compare myself to David, because he was always after God's own heart."

I laughed. "No, you're worse than Faith. And annoying."

He ignored my comment. "I want to be a preacher."

"Good for you," I said sarcastically.

"Why are you so mean?" he asked, seemingly hurt.

"You ain't seen mean. I used to beat up all the neighborhood kids . . . only because they would pick on me, but I still beat them up. I beat up they older sisters, cousins, aunties. Anyone who wanted it got it. I ain't weak. I been through hell and back and I'm still strong. You try being homeless for almost a week." I studied him, going over his soft, boyish features. He had a cute face and if he cut his hair and wore better clothes, he'd have actually been very attractive. He also seemed unconfident, innocent, and too trusting. I bet he was a virgin, too.

"You a virgin?"

His light cheeks blushed. "Um . . ."

I laughed. "You are! How old are you, Dante?"

"Eighteen."

If I had been drinking water, I would've spit it out. "You're eighteen and you're a virgin? What did your momma do, keep you locked up?"

He blinked. "Actually, she did. I went to an all-boys Catholic school until she passed away a few years ago. I graduated early and came home."

"Oh really?"

"Yeah. I felt lost and started going to different churches in search of something, and I was left empty-handed each time. But then I went to Rising Faith and listened to Pastor May preach. It was like she was talking to me. I been at that church ever since, helping her out in any way I could."

"May has a way of attracting people." I smiled. "I love her already."

"Yeah," he agreed.

"So, what do you do for fun if you don't party?"

"Read my Bible."

"Lame." I laughed. "Why are you so lame? It should be a crime."

"There are so many biblical references I could make due to that comment but I'll let it slide."

I snorted. "Good, because I was shaking in my boots."

"Sarcasm is ugly on a girl."

I stopped, dramatically gasping at his comment. I wanted to laugh but forced a straight face. "So now I'm ugly?"

"No!" He shunned himself. "No, that's not what . . . I mean, I don't think you're, um . . . you're—"

"Go ahead and say it. I have a big butt and a nice walk? You should see how I pick up men, how they drool and fall all over me."

"I wasn't gonna say you had a . . . big . . . bottom."

"But you were thinking it."

"No, I wasn't."

"All men think about it," I said as a matter of fact. "Go ahead and look at it. I'll let you get away with it just this once."

His eyes shifted, like he was trying to force himself to stare me straight in the eyes. "I will not sin."

"How is that sinning?"

"Lust."

"You can't look at my butt without lusting?"

His cheeks blushed. He was so light, he actually blushed. It was the cutest thing about him.

"Fine," I said, walking again, making sure that I twitched. I heard him sigh behind me as he caught up.

He kept his eyes straight ahead . . . on Jesus, I reckoned.

Chapter 11

I fell into a nice routine. Every day I'd go over to May's house and help her out. I'd playfully argue with Dante after his checker game with May, and after he left, I'd do more cleaning and cooking and then watch TV while May napped. Once Norma got to the house, I'd help her kids with their homework and head back to my motel.

One day, May was sitting on the porch when I arrived. She knew I was there before I even said anything. There was something joyous in her expression.

"Hey, Mrs. May. How's your back feeling today?" I asked, rubbing her shoulder and taking a seat.

"Can't complain," she said, smiling. Today, she didn't wear her shades. I studied her beautiful gray eyes. I'd wondered if they'd always been gray or if that was an effect of the beating she suffered. "I was thinking, you've been paying to stay in that motel for nearly a month. At that rate, you'll spend all of that money. Why won't you come live here at least until you're eighteen? You shouldn't be living on your own. We can get you back in school, too."

I sat back in my seat, feeling loved. Extremely loved. But the feelings of being loved never lasted long for me. Life had a way of messing that up and laughing in my face. I was afraid to get too attached to May, Norma, the kids, and even the Bible-hugging Dante. But the more time I spent with all of them, the more I loved them. They were like family and I would bathe in my happiness until the devil tried to snatch it. But there was one thing. I couldn't go to school and help May out as much as I wanted to, so I lied.

"Okay, I want to, but I dropped out of school," I told her, waiting for her to say that I couldn't stay unless I was in school.

May frowned and then nodded. "I won't press your education if it's your personal choice not to go, but I strongly encourage you to reconsider."

"Okay," I said. "Can I still stay here?"

May smiled. "Of course."

"Thank you, May! I'm so grateful."

"Don't thank me, thank God."

I hesitated, but knew it would bring her happiness to say it. I would do anything to make May happy. "Thank you, God!"

Later that morning, Dante came strutting down the street with three cans of paint and a bag full of brushes. I stood on the porch with folded arms, intrigued. When he saw me, he smiled. He always smiled.

"What's that?" I asked him.

"Paint."

"Duh, I mean what's it for?"

"The house," he said. "Wanna help me paint it?"

"The whole house?" I asked in disbelief.

"No just half of it," he said sarcastically, making me laugh. I was rubbing off on him.

"Sure."

We started on the front of the house. Dante grabbed an old boom box from the shed and turned the radio to a gospel station. Every now and then, I'd turn it to a hip hop station just to make him mad. Most of the time we just painted in silence; but every now and then, Dante would ask me about my life, and I'd always find a way to change the subject. Eventually, he got fed up.

"Why don't you ever talk about your past?"

"Because I don't like to bring it up. Why focus on the past when you can be creating a future?" I asked, stroking my brush against the house in a smooth rhythm.

"I bet it's because you used to be ratchet," he said.

I immediately stopped painting. "Where did you learn that word?"

"Some YouTube video," he said.

"Goofball. So, tell me more about yourself, Dante."

I learned that Dante was an only child. His mother was wealthy and sent him away to school at six. She remarried a few years later to a white man who had two children who were also sent away to school. Dante said he wasn't able to come home on holidays and would go at most a year without seeing his mother. His summers were great. When he got the chance to come home, his mother would take him to different parts of the world. He said his favorite place he'd visited was Israel. Once he started talking about the biblical places he'd seen, I grew bored and tuned him out.

He picked back up with telling me about his passion in music. Said he was singing before he learned how to talk. When I asked him to sing, however, he shied up and began painting silently. He told me that the day he'd sing would be the day I opened up about my past. I guessed I'd never hear him sing.

I eventually headed back inside to clean up and then headed back to the motel to get all of my belongings. May was waiting for me when I returned. She handed me a key and guided me upstairs to the first room that was always locked. She stood aside and allowed me to unlock it.

"This room ain't been used in years," she said, choking on her own words. "My youngest daughter used to stay here and help me out until she passed away ten years ago."

"How?" I put the key in the lock, but didn't open it.

"Car accident." Her words were final. I could tell she didn't want to discuss it further. We were alike in so many ways.

I nodded and opened the door. It was a beautiful room with different shades of blue. There was a queen-sized bed, two nightstands, and a small TV that sat on top of a large dresser. I walked in the room, instantly feeling grateful. I turned around to thank May, but she was already gone. I decided to unpack all of my clothes and lie in bed, and watched TV until I fell asleep.

Dante barged into my room that next morning, tears covering his face. I heard a lot of commotion below us. I sat up abruptly. Before I could even ask, Dante rushed to my side.

"It's Pastor May."

Two hours later, I sat beside Norma and Dante at the hospital waiting for the news. The doctor hadn't told us much. They only thing I knew was that Dante had come over like he did every morning to play checkers, and found May passed out on the porch, unresponsive. He immediately called the ambulance and waited for them to come. He then remembered that I was upstairs and came to get me. They wouldn't allow us to ride to the hospital with May, so we had to call Norma to come get us.

None of us really said a word to each other. What was there to say? May was an old woman, eighty-five to be exact, and could pass away at any moment. None of us were prepared for it. We'd deny the possibility until the doctor told us otherwise. But it was obvious that the thought was what was keeping us quiet.

I looked over at Norma, who clutched the chair so violently I was afraid she'd break her hand. Dante leaned forward in his chair, both hands joined together in a fist, his head hung low and his legs shaking. It felt weird to be mourning over a woman I barely came to know, but May was more than a woman. She offered me a new life that I was forever indebted to. Even though I hadn't known her long, I loved her. Now would've been a good time to pray, but I couldn't bring myself to pray to a God who'd never seemed present before. Why start now? So instead, I envisioned May walking up to us, smiling, saying she fainted due to dehydration and was okay to leave.

Eventually, the doctor came, wearing his blue scrubs and a cap to cover his hair. He smiled when he saw us. I was hoping it was a good sign. "Who is Ms. Norma Baker?"

Norma stood. "I'm Norma."

"Hi, I'm Dr. Manning."

"Is she okay?" I asked, standing up, cutting the doctor off from what he was going to say.

"She's resting now, but she'll be okay. She had a minor stroke. We ran an MRI and her brain is functioning properly. There is no damage that we can see. We'll keep her for a few days to run some more tests."

"Thank God!" Norma said, hugging Dante.

I walked up to the doctor. "Can we see her?"

"Yes, family can see her. Are you family?"

I stepped back slightly. No, I wasn't family. Disappointment stretched across my face.

"Yes, she's family," Norma said. "We all are."

The doctor nodded. "One at a time please."

I turned to Norma to show my gratification. Norma nodded, letting me know that she understood. She walked off with the doctor to see May.

Twenty minutes later, I stood before May, unsure of what to say to a sleeping woman. I pulled a chair up and sat next to her, taking her hand in mine. I hadn't realized I'd been crying until I felt the tears soak through my shirt.

"Momma May . . . that's what Norma said all your grandchildren call you. I think I'll start calling you Momma May too. You're more of a mother than my own momma." I sighed, wiping my nose with the back of my hand. "I don't think I ever thanked you for giving me a place to live, for giving me a new life. I know I've only been around for a few months, but I feel like it's been years. I think I owe you by telling you the truth. I know you can't hear me, but I'm going to practice telling you now, so that when you wake up, it'll be easier."

I stopped, gathering my thoughts. "I have a twin named Faith. She was always Momma's favorite. She got gifts for her birthday, for Christmas, and for no occasion at all. All I got were beatings and a reason for why I didn't get gifts. It was always something. Once, it was our birthday and I forgot to brush my teeth. Momma said I didn't deserve a gift because I was stupid. Only stupid people didn't brush their teeth. After that day, I started brushing my teeth four or five times a day, thinking I could earn a gift. It didn't work. Momma never noticed all of my attempts. So I stopped caring. I was angry and reckless by the time I hit my teens. I'd sneak out of the house to talk to boys. Once, I stole my sister's homecoming dress because I didn't get one. I started to blame Faith, secretly hating my own twin for Momma's actions. Faith tried to make things equal. She'd give me dresses, let me play with her toys, give me her food and say she wasn't hungry, but it still wasn't enough.

"About a year ago, Momma's boyfriend, John, started living with us. At first I didn't like him. I don't like any man I first meet. But he grew on me. He was really sweet and favored me more than Faith. I liked the attention I got from him, so fatherly, so genuine. I don't know, I guess I confused the love he had for me. I started to get a crush, thinking about him sexually, wanting him all for me. I used to fantasize about us running away together and getting married when I turned eighteen." I paused, looking at Momma May to see if she was upset yet, but her face was calm.

"I came on to him and he rejected me like any good man would, but Momma went out of town for a while, and they were goin' through some things. He was weak and I took advantage of it. We started doing it. I felt happy, alive, free. I felt like a woman. Secretly, I liked knowing what I was doing to Momma. It was a way to release all of my anger I held in for her. I wanted her to find out, to know that I was sleeping with her man. I wanted to see the pain on her face, show her what it felt like to be hurt." I paused, afraid to admit what I was about to say, afraid I would be judged. I sighed, knowing Momma May deserved the whole truth, and continued. "I got pregnant, something that had never crossed my mind. I didn't know anything about babies and the symptoms of pregnancy. I used to get sick all of the time. Well, Momma caught on and made me take a test. Everything came to light then. I told her all about the affair. I rubbed it in her face proudly. It felt like a victory.

"I told John to choose between me and Momma. I thought he would be happy that we were having a baby, but he just stood there, speechless." I choked on my own words, feeling a rush of emotion surge through me. I squeezed May's hand, needing strength to continue. "Momma laughed when John chose to stay with her, and then she beat me. She dragged me down her porch steps and kicked me out. I remember Faith just standing there, watching Momma dog me. I thought she would at least cry for me and quote the Bible. I thought she would tell me to stay strong, that God was still with me. But I don't even know if I believe in Him. Faith got to go to church when we were little. I wasn't allowed to go. The closest I got to church was under the peach tree." I sniffed. "That's why I don't like church. That's why I don't go, because I felt like God never loved me. God never came to my house to save me, why should I go to His?"

I sat there crying softly, hoping May wouldn't wake up. I could've imagined it, but I felt May tightened her grip around my hand. I could've sworn she was trying to comfort me. Perhaps that was her way of letting me know that she was there for me, even if God wasn't.

Chapter 12

Even though she was asleep, telling May about my past left me open and hurt and in need of speaking with my sister. I wanted to apologize for everything I'd ever done wrong. I hadn't stopped to think about how she was feeling about everything. I was selfish. Not only had I betrayed Momma, but I betrayed Faith. Her life was probably as ruined as mine was. And I missed her. She was a part of me that I didn't want to let go. She was my sister. It had been months since I'd last seen her.

When I got back to May's house, I went straight to the phone and called home. When Faith answered, it was a whisper. "Hello?" I wasn't able to say anything because my crying temporarily blocked my speech. "Hope? I thought I told you not to call."

"I missed you, Faith."

I heard her gasp. "After everything you did, you call to tell me that you miss me?"

"I do miss you and I'm sorry for everything!"

Faith paused, making me fear she had hung up, but then I heard her breathing. "John left. Hope, is the baby okay?"

"No, I lost it," I said barely above a whisper, but she still heard me.

"I'm sorry." She choked on her apology.

"It ain't your fault," I told her, but in a way, it was. She didn't have to tell Momma that I was pregnant by John's baby. She picked Momma over me, just like John had done.

"You're right; it's your fault. Hope, if you didn't go sleeping with Momma's boyfriend, none of this would've happened."

"I don't need you pointing fingers at me," I told her.

She sighed. "Hope, you messed my life up. You messed everyone's life up! I don't know if I can ever forgive you." She paused for a moment, and I heard commotion in the background. "I gotta go. If Momma catches me talking to you she gonna change our number. Don't call back."

"Faith! Who are you talking to?" Momma's voiced crashed through the phone and then the line dropped.

I hung up the phone, but I also hung on to Faith's last words.

Don't call back.

My sister didn't want to talk to me anymore. That fact alone hurt me more than anything Momma had ever done to me. At least I was used to Momma's rejection, but Faith's? I couldn't stomach it.

Nothing was ever going to be the same.

The next few days dragged on like a football game in overtime. While Momma May was in the hospital, Norma allowed me to stay in the house by myself. She never gave me a reason why she allowed it; maybe she didn't think about the consequences of leaving a sixteen-year-old alone in a house, especially when Dante came around. No one had to worry though. I'd never disrespect Momma May's house.

I tried to busy myself with helping Dante fix the house, anything to keep my mind off of Momma May's sickness. Dante's presence helped. We were both feeling the same way, anxious and worried, hoping the next set of tests showed nothing out of the ordinary. I missed Momma May, more than I missed my own twin. Funny how things worked like that.

Dante and I were almost finished painting the house. We came up with a plan to restore what was once beautiful about it. I took some money from my savings account and bought soil, plants, and flowers. Dante bought tools and decorations for the porch. He also bought a beautiful wind chime that sounded pure and brought peace whenever the wind shook it up. When I closed my eyes, I'd imagine a tree full of beautiful diamonds and when the wind would blow, the diamonds would slowly fall from the tree, creating that beautiful melody.

"What do you want to do with the rest of your life?" Dante's question surprised me. I looked up from the soil into his curious eyes. Unlike me, he was wearing gloves and Momma May's apron. He had a thing about germs and had no fashion sense to know how ridiculous he looked. I fought back the urge to tease him.

"Um, I ain't never thought about it." It was true. Maybe it was because I never thought a girl like me had much of a future. I thought about Faith's future and how she'd probably be a preacher's wife with at least two children and live a long, beautiful life and have plenty of grandbabies. But me? I just didn't know.

"What do you like to do?" he asked, eyeing me disgustingly as I played with the soil.

"Um, I like helping Momma May out around the house . . ."

"Then maybe you should be a nurse."

I laughed. "No, I only like helping Momma May."

Dante looked thoughtful. "Do you have any talents?"

"I guess I can sing," I told him, digging my hands deeply into the soil. I liked how soft it felt against my skin.

"Can I hear you?" he asked, but he seemed more interested with me playing in the dirt. His lips twitched, like he was holding back a laugh.

"Naw."

"Please?"

I looked at Dante. "I'll sing if you take that stupid apron and gloves off and grab that soil like a real man!"

"It's not soil." He chuckled. "It's manure."

"What's that?"

He laughed and fell backward, landing on the grass. I looked down at the soil covering my hands and arms. It had a weird smell to it that I couldn't distinguish.

"What?" I asked, watching him roll in the grass in laughter. "What is it then if it's not dirt?"

"It's . . . horse . . . poop!" he said through his laughter.

I immediately jumped up, screaming, trying everything to get the poop off of my hands and arms. I began wiping it on my clothes, and then got mad because that wasn't really effective, and all the while Dante was still on the ground, cracking up.

No wonder he wore that stupid apron.

Norma came over later that day. She had taken off of work early and had gone to the hospital to check up on Momma May. Dante was still around the house. We had watched a few movies and he'd attempted to teach me how to play checkers. Norma sat down, across from us, so that she could see us at the same time. I could tell by the tension in her shoulders and bags under her eyes that she didn't have good news.

"Momma is up and smiling. She asked about the both of you. I told her about all the work you two managed to get done in two days. She told me to tell you both that she loves you."

My heart warmed. Momma May loved me.

"And then I talked to the doctors." She sighed, rubbing her hands through her curly hair. "They said they need to keep her for a few more days, run some more tests. They said they found a tumor in her brain. They said it could be noncancerous but that they need to run more tests to be sure."

The room around me spun. I could only hear my own heartbeat, which puttered rapidly. Dante put his face in his hands and shook his head. "No," he said, standing up and pacing the room. "I'll pray."

"But it could be nothing, right?" I asked.

"Even if it's nothing, they'll still want to do surgery . . . and surgery for an old woman is risky."

"It's fine, all we have to do is pray."

I tried to ignore the fact that Dante wanted to resort to praying the first time, but now I was angry. I jumped up, turning on Dante. "Pray? You think God is going to give Momma May a miracle because you asked? Do you know how many kids die every day from cancer? I bet they mommas prayed too. And they were left with nothing but disappointment and pain! Praying ain't gonna help nothing."

Norma stood up, pointing her finger at me. "If Momma heard you talk like that, she'd have another stroke. Prayer is everything! Prayer is what got Momma beaten by that mayor and his wife instead of killed! Prayer caused Momma to be able to find a good man who took care of her and a baby that wasn't his. Maybe if you prayed more yourself, you'd see a change in your situation. You can't live in this house and not love God, girl."

"Good thing it's not your house. Momma May said I could stay here. Obviously she ain't got a problem with it," I yelled, causing Norma to step back. I'd been nothing but nice to her, who was she to judge me?

Norma shook her head. "I told Momma not to let a heathen into her house but she asked you to live here anyway. You done brought the devil with you and that's probably why Momma is sick!"

"I brought the devil with me?" I allowed the tears to flow freely. "I ain't did nothing but try to be what Momma May needed! I can't believe this bit . . . this stupid woman gonna play me like that! You don't know me to be judging me. And you ain't perfect either. You won't even tell your own grandma that her house is underwater!"

"Don't even try to turn this around on me." Tears began pouring down her face and she didn't care. She didn't even try to wipe them away. "I am trying everything I can to bring her mortgage current. What am I supposed to do?"

"I still got over half of that money Momma May gave me. You can have it back if it'll save her house," I said.

"No," Dante chimed in. "No, I overheard Norma talk to the bank before and this house been underwater for a long time! She took a second mortgage out on Pastor May's house without her knowing. It was free and clear of title! Pastor May doesn't know she owes anything!"

I turned to Norma, bewildered.

"Don't look at me like that," she said, shaking her head and twitching awkwardly. Suddenly, I noticed the bags under her eyes weren't from stress but from something else. She was good at hiding whatever it was she was hiding. So good that I thought she was an accomplished black woman. But no, there was something else eating her away, eating at her flesh. How did I not see it before? "I needed the money! My kids needed to eat. It wasn't my momma's responsibility to feed my kids! I lost my job. I didn't have any money. I hate what I did. I hate that I went behind my momma's back and put a lien on her house. And now this, more medical bills that we can't pay. Three thousand dollars down the drain! Another mouth to feed!" She paused, bending over, clutching her stomach like she was in pain. When she rose, her eyes were full of fury. "And don't either of you tell her about the mortgage. It's none of y'all's business."

"And it ain't your business where I lay my head, Norma," I said softly, feeling my own anger be replaced with worry for Momma May.

"Fine," she said. She grabbed her purse and left me and Dante to deal with the stress she placed on us both.

Dante moved to my side, caressing my back, trying to console me. I wanted to push him away, but I didn't want to hurt his feelings. Instead, I turned into him and cried.

I cried for Momma May and all of her problems. I cried for losing my twin due to my own stupidity. I cried for the baby that had once been in my stomach, who never had the chance to live and breathe. I cried for John, although he didn't deserve my tears. And I cried for myself, because there was no one who would.

I woke up around midnight. Dante's arm rested around my shoulders and I lay against him. I looked up at him, seeing that he was sleeping peacefully. I didn't really feel like moving myself. I had been surprisingly comfortable. I rested my head against his chest and fell back to sleep.

When I woke up for the second time, Dante was missing. I heard commotion coming from the kitchen and then a scream. I jumped up and ran into the kitchen and as soon as I saw what was happening, the fire alarm went off in the house. Smoke almost filled the kitchen. I ran to the back door, opening it up, fanning the room out.

Dante was standing by the oven, fanning it with an oven mitten. Inside was a plastic plate holding deformed and burnt pancakes. The plastic had melted right through the oven racks and was dripping onto the bottom of the oven. Once that dried, it would be hard to clean up. My eyes lowered as I stared at Dante. I could've killed him.

"What did you do?" I asked while fanning the fire alarm.

"I was just trying to make us pancakes." Dante opened the back door wider, allowing more of the smoke to get out.

I counted backward from ten, and said too calmly, "You don't cook pancakes in the oven."

"Well, nobody told me that."

"And you don't put plastic in the oven." I had to force the scream to subside when I finished my sentence. "The plastic is melted now! You can spend all day scraping dry plastic out of the oven all you want. Don't ask me to help. Ugh! Dante, ain't you got something better to do than sit around an old woman's house all day? Where's your friends?"

"I don't have any friends here," he said innocently.

"Probably because you're weird!" I said, storming out of the room.

"I'll forgive you for saying that."

"Whatever!"

Momma May came home that Monday, looking healthy and happy. I almost cried when I saw her. I wanted to run to her, hug her, and never let go. Norma accompanied her and didn't even dare to glance in my direction as she walked Momma May upstairs. And of course, Dante was on Momma May's other side, saying how happy he was that she was home.

Momma May stopped on the last step and turned toward me; I didn't know how she knew I was there. Maybe she felt my presence; the blind always had heightened senses. She found my face with her hand.

"My beautiful Hope." She smiled and walked inside.

It was such a small, simple gesture, but it held so much meaning. Momma May was blind. She couldn't see my outer appearance; she was referring to my heart, my soul.

Those with vision can see, but are they truly seeing? Those with hearing, are they really listening? Momma May did. She didn't need eyes to tell her what her heart could. And her true sight revealed to her that I was beautiful. Maybe I was a good person.

A lot of the unspoken tension evaporated once Momma May stepped foot in the house. All the demons that dared to threaten all of our sanity fled. There was no room for them in the house of the anointed.

Chapter 13

Winter passed by in a blur. The garden Dante and I planted in the front yard bloomed with vibrant colors. Momma May loved the new wind chime Dante had bought her. She could sit outside all day and listen to it. It was the most peaceful state of mind I'd seen her in since the doctors told us that the tumor in her brain was cancerous.

Remembering that moment and how it shattered our world was something I tried to keep deep inside. I couldn't fathom bringing it up in full details. Some things are better left unsaid.

The doctor said the cancer hadn't spread and that there may be a chance to shrink the tumor if she went through chemotherapy. Momma May rejected it, saying if it was meant for her to be healed, Jesus Himself would do it. She told us that she'd lived a full, happy life and would go willingly if Jesus called her home.

I was sitting on the porch with Momma May, listening to the sound of the wind chime and imagining a world where there was no sickness, no tears, and no pain, only laughter and joy. One where everyone had a momma like May, where there was always food on the table, where no child felt alone and unloved.

Where love and friendship were requited.

A nice black car pulled up to the curb in front of the house. I squeezed my eyes to see who it was, but the windows were slightly tinted. The driver's door opened.

Dante got out of the car, dressed in nice black dress pants, new black dress shoes, a nice light blue button-up, and a pair of expensive aviators, and his hair was freshly cut into a nice fade. The world slowed around me as he walked up to the house. My mouth hung open in shock.

He stood below the first step and took his shades off, smiling up at Momma May. "Good morning, Pastor May."

"Good morning," I said.

Dante narrowed his eyes when he looked at me. "Hope."

I narrowed my eyes back. "Dante."

"Like my new car?" he said, finally coming up the stairs.

"How did you buy a new car? You don't have a job."

"I have a trust fund my mom left me when she died. It's a lot of money."

"What's up with the new makeover?" I tried hard not to smile. Why did I want to smile anyway?

"I needed a change." His smile was bright but there was something mocking about it, like he knew I thought he was very attractive. Especially now. It irritated me, but at the same time I was impressed. "Wanna go on a joy ride?"

I looked behind him at the car and smiled. Why wouldn't a girl like me want to take a ride in a car like that? Especially next to a guy dressed like that? Who was this boy standing in front of me? It was like Dante turned into a man right before my eyes.

"Sure," I said, almost too sweetly.

Dante turned a corner with too much speed, throwing me against my door. "Slow down!" I said, gripping the dashboard. The interior of the car was just as nice as the outside. He had nice black leather seats that, he explained, had the ability to heat up when it got cold; the dashboard and radio system were clean and top notch; it even had a built-in GPS system. It also had that new car scent that I loved.

"Scared?" Dante laughed, spinning around another curb, but then he slowed down and pulled into a pharmacy. He parked the car and turned toward me.

"Hope, I have enough money to pay off Norma's mortgage on Pastor May's home and pay for her medical bills," he said. A glint of inspiration lit his eyes.

"How much money do you have?" I asked, gaping.

"More than I can count."

"And you'd pay Momma May's bills? Dante, that's—"

"The least I could do for an amazing woman who has been there for me since my mom died. You'd do the same, too."

I smiled. "I would. You got a big heart, Dante. And your swag is . . . better."

He laughed. "Come on, I gotta go pick up Pastor May's prescription."

We got out of the car and walked into the pharmacy. Dante went to the back of the store to get the medicine. I wandered around the store, looking over cosmetics and little accessories. I picked up a tube of red lipstick, wondering how I'd look in something so daring. Maybe I could use a makeover like Dante. I was still walking about in my week's worth of thrift store clothes. My pants had a hole at the bottom from wearing them so much. I could keep the money Momma May gave me since Dante was paying off her bills. Maybe I could do some more shopping of my own.

Thankfully I was able to straighten my hair with Momma May's old hot iron, or I'd be walking around with a big fro. I shook at the thought.

"Hope?"

I turned around, expecting to see Dante, but it wasn't him. I dropped the red lipstick on the floor, not bothering to pick it up as I gawked at John, who stood three feet away. He was a lot frailer than I'd remember, like he hadn't eaten a good, healthy meal in months. His clothes were bagging and oversized, his shirt had a coffee stain on it. He held some prescription medicine in his hands. I tried to make out what he was taking but couldn't. I met his stare. He almost smiled but his eyes were sad. He took a step closer and I took a step back. I came to my senses and picked up the lipstick, placing it back on the shelf with shaking hands.

"Hope, it's good to see you." His eyes darted to the ground with shame.

"Is it?" I hadn't realized I was capable of speaking. It almost sounded like someone else's voice. Someone who was scared and fragile.

He sighed, looking down at his hands, thinking of how to approach this conversation, I was sure. He looked back up at me, and then to my stomach. "How are you doing?"

"Fine."

"How is the baby?" When I didn't answer, he continued, meeting my eyes. "I've been thinking a lot about what happened. How I choked. How I made the biggest mistake of my life. Seeing your mother beat you like that—"

"And you ain't do anything to stop it."

He dropped his head again. "You're right. I wish I could take it back. I'm sorry. I . . ." He hesitated, putting one hand in his pocket. "I couldn't run away with a sixteen-year-old girl, Hope! That was the only thing holding me back. But then I thought about the baby, it's all I've been thinking about. That and how life would be now if I would've taken off with you.

"We can fix this, Hope. Me and your momma aren't together anymore. I have an apartment. It ain't much but we can fix it up really nice, decorate the baby's room. We can have our family, just like you wanted, Hope. Come with me, right now. We can raise our baby, like you always wanted. We can—"

"John!" I almost screamed, silencing him at once. There were so many things I wanted to say to him, to do to him. I thought about it all the time: what would happen if our paths ever crossed. I told myself I'd kill him, run him over. Break his legs. Tell him how bad he hurt me, how it still affected me every day. And now I had the chance, but I couldn't find the right words. All I said was, "No."

"No?" He was confused. "But I thought that's all you ever wanted."

"I was stupid."

"Hope—"

"Ain't no baby anymore. Momma killed it along with everything else. But I'm fine now . . . more than fine. Better. Stronger. Loved."

"Hope." It was Dante's voice who interrupted me. He looked from me to John and back to me again. I watched John look over Dante's nice attire and frowned. He looked back at me with questions in his eyes. "Are you okay?"

I shook my head and Dante was at my side in less than a second. He stood by me protectively.

"You got a problem?" he asked John, who paid no attention to him.

John's eyes were focused on me, waiting. "Hope," he pleaded. In a sick way, it made me feel good to see him beg for me the way I begged for him. The feeling went away as soon as it came. I still loved John and, regardless of what he did to me, I didn't want to see him hurting. He looked bent out of shape.

"Dante, can we leave now?" I kept my eyes low, doing everything I could to avoid the man who broke my heart into millions of pieces. Dante grabbed my hand and guided me to the front and outside of the door. John said nothing as we walked away. I was glad that he did.

Dante opened my car door and waited for me to get seated comfortably before shutting the door. He ran around to his side and jumped in. He started the car and sped out of the parking lot. I leaned back in my seat, thankful for the radio's music. I didn't feel like talking about what happened.

He pulled up to a nice park where beautiful trees provided shade over the bright green lawn. Kids crowded a small playground as parents sat at benches or pushed their child on swings. Couples were sprawled out on blankets, kissing and talking. Some kids flew kites while others played Frisbee with their dogs. It was a nice, family-oriented place. It almost made me feel happy. Almost.

"Come on."

Dante led me on a quiet trail that cut straight through the woods. If I had been in a better mood, I would've marveled at the nature. All of the different types of trees towering above us watched as we passed, passing secrets along in the wind. Bugs flew by, resting on nearby flowers and I could hear rodents in bushes, searching for food. It was nature at its best.

We walked in silence for some time; I supposed Dante was allowing me to cool off before broaching the subject. Surprisingly, I was ready to spill it out. Tell him everything. I needed a friend to confide in, and somehow, over the months, Dante became exactly that. A friend. Yes, he had his weird and awkward moments, but he grew on me. Some days I couldn't wait to see him, just so I could pick on him and laugh. It was what we did.

But today was different, more serious.

I didn't wait for him to ask questions. I let it all hang out.

I started by telling him about my relationship with my mom and I ended with explaining how I met Momma May. The whole time he listened and really took in everything I said. Not once did he judge me. I was grateful for that. I didn't need any more judging in my life. I'd had enough judgment to last me a century.

"So, you lost the baby." He said it more out of confirmation. "Wow. Hope, that's . . ."

"Crazy?" I laughed, although there was nothing funny about it. Maybe I did it to lighten the mood. "I know."

"I really think you should talk to Pastor May, confess it all to her and listen to what God tells you through her. You think God doesn't love you because your mom never did, but that's a lie. God said He will never forsake you."

"I know what God says, I just have a hard time believing it."

"Talk to Pastor May, she'll help you. Maybe that's why God placed you two on the same path, for confirmation. Maybe God knew you'd need someone who understands you to help you come to Him."

"Maybe," I said. I felt exhausted. Too many emotions. "Can we go back to the car now? I'm tired. I want to go home and take a nap."

"Sure."

Dante led me back to the car. We sat in silence on the way home. Somewhere along the ride, I fell asleep. I didn't feel Dante as he parked in front of the house but I felt him lift me up and carry me inside. I should've told him that I was awake, but there was something about being in a man's arms as he carried me.

Dante sat me gently on my bed and kissed my forehead. I didn't stir as he lay down beside me and dozed off as well. Good thing Momma May was blind, because she would've caught a case seeing how we ended up napping in the same bed. I was glad that Dante lay next to me. Somehow he knew it wasn't wise to leave me alone in my current state. For that, he was a great friend.

I woke up first, turning toward a snoring Dante. He was calm; he was at peace. I took the time to study his face. He had long black lashes and touched his cheeks as he slept. He had small brown freckles on his nose that I'd never noticed before. I smiled, noticing the drool escaping out of the corner of his mouth.

I decided to mess with him. I plugged his nose until a loud snore erupted from his mouth. His hand shot straight up and I moved my hand away as he rubbed his nose and settled back into a deep sleep. I waited a few seconds before I did it again, making him jump this time. I buried my face in my pillow and laughed. I looked over at him still sleeping. I raised my hand again, but his hand quickly sliced through the air and caught mine. His grip was tight.

"Don't," he said and opened his eyes. I laughed so hard, pulling out of his grip, turning on my back. Dante sat up, rubbing his eyes with a smile on his face. He looked out of the window to the dark sky. "What time is it?"

"After eight. We missed dinner. We should order pizza."

He sighed. "I can't. I gotta get home."

He suddenly seemed distant, distracted. He quickly jumped out of bed and walked over to the door, putting his shoes on.

"Okay. How about tomorrow?" I asked, turning on my side and placing a hand under my head for support.

He didn't look at me. He seemed to be avoiding eye contact. "I'm not coming over tomorrow."

"The next day?" I frowned. Since when did Dante not come over?

"Maybe," he said, and left the room, shutting the door behind him. I didn't even get a good-bye. That was strange even for him. I lay back on my back, wondering what I could've done to chase him away like that.

Chapter 14

Momma May was in a great mood that next morning. I was awakened by the sound of gospel music exploding through the radio. I got dressed and headed downstairs and found her in the living room dancing in place. She didn't hear me come into the room over the radio. I took a seat on the coach and watched until she grew tired.

"Good morning," I said, watching her jump, scaring her half to death. Her laughter was childlike.

She took a seat on the couch. "An old lady's gotta find a way to work out."

I nodded, half listening. I had a lot on my mind due to Dante's weird departure. I couldn't stop wondering if I had done something wrong. Putting this morning's episode behind me for the time being, I focused on what I wanted to talk to Momma May about.

"Momma May," I began, but I quickly choked on my words. "Dante said I should talk to you about God, because I can't come to terms with"—I took a breath before continuing—"with everything."

She nodded, sitting back comfortably on the couch. "Well, let me ask you this, do you believe in God?"

I sighed, lowering my head. "I don't know."

"What do you think makes you question His existence?"

"I don't know. I guess because I was never given the opportunity to have a personal relationship with Him. I never got to experience Him firsthand. I had to hear about Him through Faith." I sighed. "And I feel like, if God loves me, why did He give me such a messed-up life?"

Momma May nodded. "God works in mysterious way, baby. I can't begin to give you an answer, but I can give you some insight based on what I've been through." She sighed, sitting back in her seat. "After I lost my sight, I felt lost and alone and there was no one there to guide me. How could I find a place to live if I couldn't see? Everything became a dark place.

"I used to love to draw, but how could I draw if I couldn't see what I was drawing? I'd lost everything, but God picked me up. He told me to have faith in Him and He'd be my eyes. He'd guide me to where I needed to get. I fought with Him, not wanting to submit to His will, wanting to rely on my own failing strength. 'God!' I said. 'Why me?' Do you want to know what He said? He said, 'Why not?" I didn't understand what He meant for a long time.

"After the mayor beat me blind, I walked for three days straight, not knowing where He was taking me. But faith is walking blindly on God's path, relying solely on Him. I questioned Him along the way. Fought with Him, denied Him, but I didn't leave His path. Eventually a young man named Curtis Baker found me passed out and dehydrated. He took me in, fed me, gave me water, and nursed me back to health. He was a preacher. A fine speaker. He was after God's own heart. That's the kind of man you want, one after God's own heart."

I thought about what Dante once told me, how he compared himself to David because David was after God's own heart. The thought warmed me inside. I thought I knew a good man. I thought John was one, and maybe he was, in his own way, but he wasn't after God's own heart. He was for himself.

"Do you know how it felt when I had my first born, knowing I'd never be able to look at her face, see her smile, see her take her first step? I didn't even know what

Curtis looked like. I didn't get the chance to have those memories. I started doubting God again. He said a just man falls seven times. And girl did I fall. I'd get depressed and blame God. I thought it was His fault. He could've stopped the mayor and his wife from finding me. He could've provided me shelter like He did to so many men in the Bible. But He didn't. I felt unloved." I understood exactly what Momma May felt like, to be unloved.

"I thought being blessed was living a great life with no problems, no pain. But I was wrong. Being blessed is exactly the opposite. I think I know why God allowed me to be blind. I was too proud, too exalted. I didn't stop and just listen to Him and His will. So He put me in a position where I had no choice but to rely on Him. It was the best thing He could've ever done."

"So you think He purposefully blinded you so that you'd be obedient? I thought He gave us our own will."

"He does. See, God knows our moves before we even make them. He knew that the mayor and his wife were out to get me. He didn't interfere with their will. God doesn't stop an angry man from hurting the innocent. Afterward, He lifts the innocent and weak up and makes them stronger. He brings good out of even the worst situations. People blame God for their misfortune, but they forget to praise Him once He brings them out of it. It's not God's fault. That's what I learned. The only thing He did was picked me up and gave me a better life.

"And now I have a praise and a testimony far greater than the pain I once had. Hope, don't blame God. Look at what He's done for you. He gave you a new home, a new family who loves you, a new Hope. Look at yourself in the mirror and tell me that you're the same girl who was starving, hungry, and helpless. You can't. Even I see the growth in you, and I'm a blind old lady. God has brought you through."

When I exhaled, it felt like the weight of the world lifted off of my shoulders. It felt as if I had been holding my breath for a lifetime. When I inhaled, the air was cool and crisp. I felt a strange, satisfying sensation spread through my chest. It felt like spring, like pure light and spirit coursing through me. I fell from the couch onto my knees and began crying. I lifted my hands and screamed, *"Jesus!"*

"Yes, yes, yes!" Momma May praised. "Oh, Lord, oh, Jesus, bless this child who needs you more than ever. Show her the way to you, Father. In Jesus' name, allow her to see your love. Allow her to be saved by the blood of Jesus! Oh, Lord Jesus! Yes! Allow your holy spirit to rest upon her as you forgive her of her sins. And as you forgive her, allow her to forgive those who've sinned against her. Allow her to place her past behind her and move into her destiny, Lord! Thank you, Jesus!"

We stayed that way for what seemed like hours, crying and praising God as I finally accepted Him into my heart.

Dante didn't come around for a few days. I felt anxious without him near. It was almost like I used him as a crutch. Whenever I was bored, I'd pick on him. Whenever I was happy, I'd laugh with him. Whenever I needed to busy myself to keep my demons at bay, I'd do housework with him. Momma May didn't have anyone to play checkers with, and so I had to learn. After a few games, I got the hang of it.

"How can you play checkers when you can't see?" I hoped my question didn't offend her.

"You see the dots on the pieces? It's brail. Dante got it specially made for me. Plus I memorize my moves. I know which pieces are mine and which are his. You'd be surprised to know all the things you can still do when blind."

I smiled. "Dante is faithful to you."

"When his mom died, he was lost. God used me to help him find his way again," she said matter-of-factly.

"Why he ain't been around lately?"

"Dante's mom passed away around this time a few years ago. He doesn't take it so good. He does this every year, but he usually comes around after a few days."

I nodded, relieved. "I thought I did something wrong."

And then it occurred to me. Maybe Dante slept in my bed that evening because it was he who didn't want to be alone. When he woke up, he realized it was the day his mom passed away and rushed out of my room.

"No," Momma May said. "That boy admires you."

"You think?" I asked, smiling.

"Oh, I know. You're all he talks about when we're playing checkers."

I laughed and decided to change the subject. It was an awkward conversation to have with an old woman. I also wasn't ready to accept the possibility of Dante liking me.

"How did his mom die?"

"Suicide."

I gasped, knocking over all of the checker pieces. I bent over, picking them all up, shunning myself. "I'm sorry," I said. "You was gonna win anyway."

"Hey, Momma!"

I hadn't realized Norma was on the porch until she spoke. I looked up at her, noticing her relaxed and almost happy smile. There was still something unnerving about her but I couldn't put my finger on it. I placed all of the checker pieces on the board and stood.

"Hope, can I talk to you for a minute?"

"Yeah," I said and then turned to Momma May. "I'll be back."

Norma led the way into the kitchen and took a seat. I sat across from her and waited for her to speak. I didn't forget about the last conversation we had, the one where she admitted to placing a second mortgage on Momma May's home. I wondered how long she had before the home foreclosed. I hoped Dante had already paid it off. How could she do that to her own grandmother? How could she go behind the most amazing woman's back and steal her identity to get a mortgage? But then I remembered the things I did to my momma, how I slept with her man. I wasn't the one to judge.

"Dante came by with a check to pay off the mortgage. They're processing the lien release and said it would take a few weeks to a month to be free and clear," she said.

"And you're telling me this because . . . ?"

"I figured you'd want some peace of mind and I figured we could keep this between the three of us, pretend it never happened," she said with a hushed voice.

"But it did happen." I sighed. "I ain't a snitch. I am gonna tell you how I feel, though."

"I don't need backlash from a child." She snorted.

"It ain't backlash, it's the truth. And you should feel bad that a child would even feel the need to tell a grown woman about herself. What does that say about you? Momma May could've lost everything she spent her life trying to build. It ain't nothing but the grace of God that allowed Dante to pay the loan off."

Norma gave me a puzzled look. "So you believe in God now?" She almost laughed. I wanted to hit her, but the good Lord stopped me.

"I do. Well, I'm getting there," I told her. "Thanks to Momma May. And don't try to turn this around on me."

Norma stood up, clutching her purse close. "Look, I gotta go to work. I'm late. I don't have time for this."

"Yup." I watched her storm out of the kitchen. She was the type of woman who would never learn from her own mistakes.

Momma May and I spent the rest of the day bonding. She told me stories about her husband while I brushed her long silver hair. She had some good memories. Some were so funny I fell to the ground in tears, laughing. And then she told me about one of the best days of her life: her wedding day.

"I was so nervous," she began. "One of our friends had sewn me a nice, beautiful dress, but at that time I was pregnant with my first, and so the dress didn't fit. My husband told me to cut a big hole in the belly."

"Did you?"

"No! Half the things that came out of that man's mouth was nonsense. My wedding dress was a gift from God, but I'll tell you about that story later. Did I ever tell you that I've been living in this house since we married? We lived a good life together. We had two beautiful girls and couldn't ask for more. He was a great father, always there for his family. A true man of God." Her eyes saddened. "When he passed away, I didn't know how I'd manage. I spent many months fasting and praying. I thought our church we built would fall apart, but God didn't let that happen. I took my husband's place and became the pastor. I didn't think people would follow a woman, but they did. I got our church back on its feet and kept preaching the Word of God. People came from all over the country to hear the blind woman preach."

"How did he pass away?"

Momma May closed her eyes, revisiting the memory. "Car accident, Christmas of 1978. He was hit by a drunk driver coming home from a late night at the church. I was sitting at home with my grandbabies, wrapping gifts for friends and family. They wanted to open one present, which was a tradition passed on to them from their parents. I told them to wait for Grandpa to come home. There was a knock on the door. The girls jumped up, excited, thinking it was Grandpa, but I was thinking why would he knock when he had a key? I got up and went to the door. It was the police. They told me about the accident, said my husband died on the way to the hospital.

"Losing the love of your life is the hardest thing one will ever have to go through. I felt like I lost half of myself. I wouldn't wish it on anyone. God took away my true love, but He brought new ones here. You and Dante ain't the first kids to come to my doorstep. From the eighties until now, God blessed me to be able to help out kids who were around your age. They'd come to the church, lost and needing love, and God allowed me to shower them with it. It was my calling, to love those who knew no love. God is an awesome God."

"And you're an awesome woman," I told her. "I'm so grateful for everything, Momma May."

"Don't thank me, baby. Thank God."

Dante showed up the next day, looking happy, greeting us like he hadn't been missing for days. I understood why he did it, but it hurt knowing that he hadn't told me. He shut me out. I'd opened up to him about my life, my past, and he couldn't even let me in. Maybe I didn't deserve it or hadn't earned it. I couldn't expect him to open up to me just because I confided in him. But I was still disappointed.

"Hey, Hope." I turned away from him, ignoring him. "What's wrong?"

"I'm gonna get something to drink, you want anything?" I asked Momma May.

"I'm fine, baby," Momma May replied.

I stood up, bumping Dante's shoulder as I went inside. He followed. I went to the refrigerator, dramatically swinging the door open. I grabbed a can of soda and shook it up. Dante stared at me like a lost puppy.

"Hope, what did I do?"

I turned around, burning holes in his eyes. "I opened up to you about everything! Things I ain't even told Momma May when she was conscious. But I told you! And what do you do? You comfort me the whole evening, making me feel special, and then in the morning, you take off running. I thought I did something wrong! I ignored the hurt I felt for three days!"

"Hope, it wasn't you."

"Oh, I know now because I had to hear it from Momma May!" I continued shaking up the can of soda with fury. "She told me about your mom passing away. Well, why ain't you tell me yourself?"

"Because—"

"Wrong answer! Let me show you how I feel about you right now." I faced the can of soda toward him and opened it. The drink sprayed all over his clothes, soaking him. He gasped, taking a step back.

I watched him, soaked and shocked. He didn't know what to do with himself and I couldn't hold the anger any longer. Seeing him standing there looking crazy, my anger quickly turned into laughter. I fell on the floor, laughing so hard my stomach knotted. Dante ended up following suit and collapsed beside me, laughing just as hard. Our laughter didn't subside for minutes.

"I'm sorry, Dante. I was so mad," I said, pulling myself up to sit against the refrigerator.

"I should be angry right about now," he said, licking soda off of his fingertips. "If I'm gonna be sticky, you will be too."

Before I could fully register what he meant, he leaped at me, wrapping his arms around my waist and pushing himself against me so that I could get wet. I screamed, trying to pull away, but he had me locked. He was stronger than I thought.

And then he kissed me. His lips were soft against mine, causing butterflies to go crazy inside of my stomach. I thought about running my hands through his hair, pulling him closer and tasting more of him, but the kiss ended all too quickly as he rushed to his feet, backing away. "I'm sorry," he said, blushing wildly. I stood up, walking up to him, shaking my head. "I'm so—"

And then my mouth was on his, tasting the soda on his lips, pulling him as close as he could get, wrapping my arms around his shoulders.

"What's all the hollerin' for?"

Dante and I froze in our passionate kiss. Our eyes darted to Momma May, who stood just outside of the kitchen. I slowly pulled away from Dante, straightening my shirt. Momma May took a step in the kitchen, inches away from stepping in the soda.

"No!" I shouted. "Don't come into the kitchen! Dante spilled soda!"

"Me?" Dante whispered, amused that I'd throw him under the bus.

"I mean, I spilled it . . . on him. It's everywhere, like a murder scene."

"Okay, clean it up," Momma May said, walking away. "And stop kissing in my kitchen. I could hear you two smooching from the front porch!"

Chapter 15

I turned to Dante, whose cheeks were rose red from the kiss. He opened the back door and stepped onto the back porch. He leaned against the railing, trying to get some air. I followed him outside, watching as he bent over the railing as if in pain.

"Lord, please forgive me," he said.

I folded my arms, slightly offended for the apology to God and headed back inside. Why did he feel the need to apologize? It was a kiss! A simple, almost meaningless, caught-in-the-moment kiss! What was the big deal? It felt like a heap of cold, bitter rejection. I sighed and stormed back into the house.

Why did I care? It wasn't like I liked Dante in that way. If anything, I thought him to be weird and a little annoying. But to like him? No. I didn't. Not in that way. So then why was I trying to convince myself that I didn't?

I walked onto the front porch, took a seat next to Momma May, and closed my eyes, listening to the sound of nature all around me. Something about it soothed me, made me feel whole. But not today. I still had a case of anxiety. I squeezed my eyes shut tighter, but nothing. I was still thinking about Dante. The kiss. How I really felt about it.

"Why you over there breathing all hard?" Momma May asked. "Probably because of all the kissing in my kitchen!"

"I'm sorry, Momma May."

"Don't apologize." She smiled. "Love doesn't need an apology."

I sat up in my chair. "Love?" I laughed. "No, I don't love Dante. It was a mistake, a moment of . . ." I sighed. "It's weird talking to you about it."

"If you can't talk to me, who can you talk to?" She was right. "How is your walk with Jesus coming along?"

Well, I hadn't really been walking with the Lord. That day after I felt His presence, I hadn't really given much thought to it again. I didn't know what to do. I was still my same self. "Not good," I admitted.

"And why is that, baby?"

I sighed. "I don't know. I just ain't thought about it. I got too many things going on in my mind."

"Do you want to be closer to God?"

"I guess."

"Do you want to know Jesus personally?"

"Yes."

"Jeremiah 4:3: 'For thus saith the Lord to the men of Judah and Jerusalem, Break up your fallow ground, and sow not among thorns.' Do you know what that means? Well, it could mean different things to different people at different times. But in this case, the fallowed ground is your past hurt. How can we have a close relationship with God if our lives are being controlled by past pain and regret? How can we experience Him if we stay distant? First, you need to break up all of the negative and hurtful things keeping you from God. The root is damaged. Nothing can be fruitful if the root is dead. So you have to fix the underlying cause of what's keeping you away from God. Also, He says, 'sow not among thorns.'

"Picture planting a garden around thorns. Once the flowers start to bloom, they get bruised by the nearby thorns and die. So once you dig up all of the pain and hurt that's keeping you from God, you have to move out of that place of thorns and into a clear, protected place. Do you understand?"

I thought about what she said. "Not really."

"God wants you to fix the root of the problem and then move into a better position so that you can be fruitful and have a relationship with Him. You believe in Jesus now, you've repented, but you haven't changed. You can't change, either, not until you break up your fallow ground and sow not among thorns. Get rid of those negative thoughts, worldly pleasures, forgive those who hurt you, stay away from the things that tempt you to backslide, and begin building your relationship with God on better grounds."

"And what if I can't?"

"You are already on better grounds," she told me. "What you need to do now is pray."

I was instantly frustrated. "Everyone says pray, but I don't understand why we have to pray. What good is it when nothing ever changes?"

"I've told you this before. Prayers never go unanswered. God knows what we need before we even begin praying. He's already made up His mind on how to answer. Tell me one thing you've prayed about that wasn't answered."

"A pretty dress. Faith always used to get dresses, but I got nothing."

"God could've been telling you not to pray for the dress, but pray for love. If your mother would've loved you, she would've automatically gotten you dresses. Sometimes we ask the wrong things in prayers, which can cause them to seem unanswered, but your prayers weren't. God's answer was simply 'no' or 'wait.' Hope, take time every morning when you wake up and pray to God. Pray for you to be able to break up the fallowed ground, forgive those who hurt you, and to grow closer to Him."

"And what if I can't forgive?"

She smiled. "Pray for God to give you the strength to do so. Hope, prayer is the cure for everything."

Just then Dante appeared from the side of the house and stood in the grass below us. He avoided eye contact with me as he spoke with Momma May. "I'm going home now, Pastor May."

I stood up, fuming. "But you just got here."

"I know." He still avoided eye contact.

My anger grew like a wildfire, threatening to destroy everything in my path. I stomped down the porch steps with my hands on my hips and faced Dante, who seemed uncomfortable to have me so close.

"Oh, what's wrong now, Dante?" My voice took on a sarcastic edge that made him back away. "You was just kissing me a few minutes ago and now you acting brand new. I got cooties now?"

"We disrespected Pastor May's house . . . and Jesus."

"You're worse than my sister! I'm tired of all you Bible-hugging Jesus freaks! You know what, Dante, you couldn't even have me if you tried. Or probably any woman for that matter! Why? Because you hide behind your Bible and use it as an excuse for why you shouldn't do normal things, like kiss! But deep down, you're just afraid of women. You ain't been around one your whole life. Your momma just gave you off. You probably feel like other women will give up on you too, so you run scared like a little bit—"

"*Enough!*" Momma May's voice broke through the air, silencing me immediately. I turned around, looking at the glorious woman leaning over the porch railing, looking larger than life. I felt small beneath her. "Dante is a fine young man who will make his wife proud one day. Who are you to demean him? Belittle him for his own beliefs that you now share? Not once has that boy said anything bad about you. But you want to get upset over childish things? He's right, y'all shouldn't be kissing in my house! He got enough sense to feel like he disrespected me.

But you? Child, you got a long way to go. I thought our conversation helped you some but you just went right back to that bitter, angry, mad-at-the-world attitude! Don't take it out on Dante, take it out with Jesus. Only He can help you."

I stared dumbfounded at Momma May as my anger dissolved. She was right. I had no reason to get angry because he felt bad about disrespecting Momma May and God. If anyone should've felt bad, it should've been me. I had figured it wasn't a big deal, because Momma May and I had a conversation about it afterward. She didn't sound upset then. Maybe it was because she started preaching to me. Either way, I was wrong. I didn't think about how God would feel. I was so used to keeping Him at a distance, I hadn't taken time to learn the things that He thought were sinful. I turned to Dante to apologize, but he was already pulling off.

When evening came, I busied myself with cooking dinner and cleaning. Anything to keep my mind off of Dante. Momma May had given me a long lecture about my actions. Although very annoying, it was needed. I ended up feeling bad about the things I had said to Dante. I picked up the phone three times, attempting to call him, but my stubbornness won over. I ended up hanging up each time.

The next day, I did what Momma May said. I sat up in my bed, feeling empty and angry, like most mornings. I took in a deep breath and began to pray. "Jesus, Momma May said I should start praying every morning to you, that it's gonna help me get closer to you. She said I got a lot of anger on my heart that I need to let go. I don't know how I'm gonna do that. I hate too many people, been hurt too many times. I think the only way I could forgive them is by pretending it never happened. But that's wrong too, right? Why does it seem like everything I do is wrong?

Well, I pray that you'll help me to forgive . . . hopefully soon."

Dante's car pulled up next to the curb and he jumped out with a new purpose and a smile on his face. Momma May had just taken a seat on the porch, which was where she spent most of her mornings. I stood right inside of the screen doors with my arms folded, putting up my usual defensive pose, waiting for his rejection.

He skipped up the stairs with a soft smile and said hello to Momma May and then he stood before me. His goofy smile didn't waiver. I felt my own lips twitch as I tried to hold my own smile in.

"So . . ." He shifted awkwardly. "Want to learn how to drive?"

My eyes widened as I looked past him to his car and then to Momma May. "I thought you was mad at me."

He shrugged. "So I guess you don't want to drive then." He turned halfway around before I stopped him.

"Fine! I want to."

Ten minutes later we were at the beginning of a quiet street. The road looked about a mile long and had no major turns or intersections that would scare me. Dante parked the car on the side of the street and switched seats with me. Once I was behind the wheel, I felt invisible, free, like I had control over my life.

Once I learned how to drive, I could use the money Momma May gave me to get a car and then I could begin working part time until I saved up enough money to move out of Momma May's house. Before Dante could say anything, I slammed on the gas, jerking the car forward. Dante flew back in his seat.

I could barely control the wheel, causing the car to sway from side to side. Dante grabbed a hold of the wheel and jerked it left, causing us to miss a trashcan.

"Hit the brakes!" he yelled and I slammed on the brakes, causing him to jerk forward. Once the car was stopped, I heard nothing but his deep breaths. His chest was heaving dramatically. I felt my own adrenaline kick in.

"Oh my God! That was so fun! Let's do it again."

"No!" The word flew out of his mouth with a rush of breath. I waited for him to compose himself. "Hope, you're crazy. Do you have a death wish? Why did you do that?"

"You said I could drive."

"Not like that! You don't drive like that. You put your foot on the gas very slowly, and the same with the brakes. And you don't swerve! You try to keep the wheel straight!"

"Well why didn't you tell me that?"

"You didn't give me a chance to!" He sighed. "Just try again . . . and please don't kill me."

After multiple attempts at driving a straight line, I finally managed to do it decently, although Dante was still on edge until I was once again in the passenger seat. He pulled over on the side of the road, too anxious to drive due to the exciting events of my driving lesson. I took the silence as a way to gain access to his personal thoughts of me.

"Dante, why ain't you mad at me?"

He looked over at me. "Pastor May told me to let it go, that you didn't mean anything. Plus, the Bible teaches us that we should forgive those who wrong us."

I thought back to what Momma May was telling me about my past. How I should let it go, forgive. But how do you forgive the very thing that keeps you tossing and turning each night? The thing that makes you who you are, that shaped your thoughts? How do you forgive the person who should've loved you the way a mother should? It was a pain that would be carried until death and maybe even after. "Can you teach me how to forgive?"

Dante frowned. "I don't know how to do that. It's something that begins within. Nobody can teach you that. You have to find it inside. But it's somewhere in there." He pointed at my heart. "Maybe you need to go back to the source that caused you the pain and face it. Sometimes knowing that you're better than the situation helps." Dante put the car in drive and pulled off. "I need to stop at the store before I take you back home."

Home.

I once thought I knew the meaning of that word. I thought home was where the family was, where Momma and Faith lived. But I now realized that the place where Momma lived was nothing but a house. I now had a home, one that made me feel loved, one that taught me right from wrong, one that only encouraged me to be better than I was. I felt secure.

Dante pulled up at a small store. We walked inside, joking and teasing each other. Dante went to the food section, looking over different meats and breads. He handed me a few items to put in the basket.

"What's this stuff for?"

He turned to me with a wide smile. "Picnic."

I felt a surge of jealousy rush through me. Who was he going on a picnic with? He never told me about a girl. The thought made me feel weird. I was only ever jealous of Faith.

"For who?"

Dante laughed at my expression. "For us. Pastor May said we need to get out of the house, get some air. So I decided to do a picnic. Looks fun in the movies."

"Ain't picnics for white people? Oh, wait." I started laughing. Dante was the whitest black man I'd ever met. Even more so than John. John was just proper because of his workplace, but Dante grew up in a predominately white boys school. He had no hope of surviving in the hood.

"Funny, let's go," I said, heading toward the cash register so that Dante could check out.

As Dante drove to the park, I glared out of the window at the passing houses. I wondered what it meant to go on a picnic, if it qualified as a date or if it was simply us just having fun. I wanted to ask him his opinion on the picnic but decided against it. I was sure he didn't intend for me to take it as him wanting to have a date. He did say it was Momma May's idea and that he thought it looked fun in the movies. I was over-thinking things.

Once he found a parking space at the park, I quickly got out and headed straight for the nature trail. I didn't realize how fast I had taken off until Dante called out to me. I slowed, allowing him to catch up. He was barely managing to carry all of the picnic goods and so I took the blanket that looked as if it was about to fall. Dante caught my eyes; his expression was a mix between inquiry and amusement.

"My bad," I said, exhaling deeply. I closed my eyes, trying to change my thoughts, which somehow managed to go haywire on the way to the park. After I cleared away the thoughts about the "picnic date," I started thinking about Momma and John.

The last time I saw John, he mentioned how he and Momma was no longer together. I wondered if what happened between him and me eventually caused their relationship to fall apart. There was a time in my life where I would've laughed at the thought, but I realized a new emotion, one more prominent. A feeling I had felt for a while but was just now accepting. Regret.

I'd felt it when I talked on the phone with Faith, I'd felt it when I told Momma May everything I'd done, and I'd felt it when I walked away from John in the store.

"Are you good?" Dante asked, putting his free hand on the back of my shoulder.

"Yeah, I'm good."

The park was beautiful and full of nature trails and playgrounds. There was an area for events that had a stage for performances and concerts, and an area for family reunions and cookouts. Dante explained that on the east side of the park there was a large lake for canoeing and fishing, but he preferred a more desolate location. We headed off in that direction.

After a few minutes of walking, Dante and I slowed and sat down at the edge of a small lake. A few ducks swam about, adding to the serene picture before me. The sun was high in the sky, casting warm rays of love, causing me to almost feel okay.

Dante and I laid down the blanket and sorted the food, plastic plates, and cups. He had turkey meat, bread, cheese, lettuce, and tomatoes for sandwiches, and pickles, soda, and chips for a snack.

I took a seat facing the lake and felt Dante take a seat next to me. His shoulder brushed mine. He grabbed my hand and put it in his, gently caressing the length from my knuckles to my wrist. It was as if he knew I needed some sort of affection. Dante must've been able to tell because of how my shoulders had been tensed and how quiet I had been. His gesture caused my tears to pour. I was sure the ducks would've been pleased to swim in my sorrow.

"It's okay, Hope."

"You don't know that," I spat.

"Ten minutes ago, you were fine. What happened between then and now?" he asked.

"My thoughts happened," I explained. "My past always haunts me, no matter how good my day is going."

"Sounds like you need to deal with your past," Dante pointed out.

"Naw, really?" I stated sarcastically. "I know what I need to do. I just don't know how to do it."

"Pray and have faith in God. He promises us that—" Dante began, placing his hand on top of mine.

"He promises a lot of stuff I ain't seen." I sighed, cutting him off. "He promised He wouldn't put more on me than I can handle. Faith told me that. And guess what, I can't handle it! It's too much."

"If it was, you would be dead," he simply said.

I looked down at our hands touching and turned to Dante. "Do you care about me?"

His light cheeks reddened but he didn't hesitate. "Yes."

"Then why did the kiss make you spazz out?"

He shifted, seemingly uncomfortable. "I never kissed a girl, for one." I laughed but he kept talking. "And I don't want to lust. It's a sin."

"One that can be forgiven."

"It's not right to play with God, to sin and think God will still forgive us. We need to try our hardest to not sin, truly repent . . . and I did. Plus, we disrespected Pastor May's house."

"Okay, I get it, you're by the book. You're a one-of-a-kind black male." I picked up a pickle and bit into it, thankful my tears were now gone. "So, do you ever think about losing your virginity, or is the thought a sin too?"

He smiled. "Yes, lusting in your mind is a sin because it leads to fornication. And I'll lose my virginity one day . . . when I'm married."

"What?" I was appalled. "What if you don't ever get married?"

He shrugged. "Then I'll be a virgin for life."

"What if I took your virginity?" I watched his face redden as he registered what I said. I scooted closer, removing my hand from his to caress his shoulder. "I could seduce you. I'm good at that. And then God can only be mad at me."

He scooted away. "No, it doesn't work like that."

I scooted closer to him and began placing kisses on his neck. I didn't know what came over me. Maybe it was as simple as being a hormonal teenager. I was trying to seduce a second victim, and for what? My own personal enjoyment in making him a man? Pride? Loneliness? Maybe it was all of the above.

But Dante was stronger than John, maybe because of Jesus. He gently pushed me away and stood up. The rejection angered me, reminded me of Momma's rejection. I stood up, barely containing my anger.

"Dang, Dante, you gay?"

"No." He almost laughed but it was obvious he was battling something inside. He looked conflicted the way his eyebrows furrowed.

"Yeah, you is. Can't no man resist me."

"A man strongly rooted in his religion can." He sighed, and ran his hand through his hair. "Don't even try to get mad, Hope."

"I can if I want to." I folded my arms stubbornly.

"You're childish and selfish."

"So?"

"It's not attractive," he stated.

"Lames ain't attractive either," I said accusingly but Dante just shrugged.

"If you're not attracted to me and yet try to seduce me, that makes you desperate for love," Dante said.

His last words hit deep. I didn't have a comeback. It was true. It was the reason I had seduced John in the first place. It was the reason I stole Faith's dress. It was the reason I wanted to be close to Momma May and now the reason I tried to seduce Dante. I was desperate for love. I'd do anything for it.

"Hope," Dante began.

"Don't talk to me," I said as he tried to console me. He knew his words hit something deep inside, causing me pain. I would've moved away from him, but I was stuck in a stupor.

"If you really want love, and you're desperate for it, try finding it in God. Redirect your passion unto Him. He will satisfy it. I thought you had a breakthrough that day you talked to Momma May and accepted Jesus."

"I did accept God, but that don't mean all my problems went away."

"Hope, when you accepted Him, it means you have to begin to rely on Him. That's why you need to read your Bible. It tells you how to handle situations. You need to pray so that God can help you."

"Why does everybody throw God in my face?"

"To help you, but you keep rejecting it. How do you expect to get better if you aren't taking your medicine?"

I snorted. "My medicine?"

"The Word. It satisfies you more than bread. It helps you stay focused on God. It—"

"Ugh!" I groaned. "Stop preaching to me! I just . . . I just wanna go home. Take me home, Dante."

I started walking back in the direction we came from, making sure to keep a big gap between us. I didn't want to hear his Jesus banter. I wanted to be alone.

Twenty minutes later, Dante pulled up to the curb and I jumped out before the car completely stopped. I almost lost my balance but didn't care. I stormed up to the house, noticing Momma May was inside. She'd probably fallen asleep on the couch. Dante followed slowly, keeping a good distance between us. I didn't care. I just wanted to bury myself deep in my covers and sleep the rest of the day away.

I opened the screen door and stepped through. Everything was normal. The TV was turned to the usual soap operas and Momma May was asleep on the couch. I smiled at the sight and went up to my room. I plopped down on my bed and closed my eyes.

And embarrassment hit me.

I threw myself at Dante. Dante, who was a nerd. Dante, who was a virgin. Dante, who was a Jesus freak. He rejected me. It did numbers to my ego. But did I even like him? I laughed at the thought. No, he just happened to be there. I was not attracted to him. Or was I? I did care what he thought of me. How he smiled when he saw me. I noticed the little things about him. He was caring, sweet, innocent, and ungrudging. He should have been everything that I wanted. And I threw myself at him, recklessly, ruining any chance I may have had. But did I even want a chance?

I shook the thought out of my head.

"Hope!" Dante's loud scream broke my reverie. I sat up, wondering if I had imagined it. "Hope! Help!"

I jumped out of the bed and darted downstairs. I was greeted by the sight of Dante, checking Momma May's pulse. He looked up at me standing frozen and unsure.

"Is she . . ."

"She's breathing, but barely," he said, although his voice was deceiving. "Call the ambulance, Hope!"

I couldn't move. My eyes were glued to Momma May's seemingly lifeless figure. My heart ran rapid inside of my chest and my eyes watered, daring to explode with a river of tears. Dante looked up at me, his eyebrows furrowed. "Call them! Now!"

His angry voice brought life back into my limbs and I ran for the phone, calling the ambulance, praying that Momma May would live to see another day.

Chapter 16

I would explain the rush of paramedics who burst through the house and how they carried Momma May away. I would explain how Dante and I even got to the hospital, waiting room, all of the in-between emotions, but everything passed by in a blur. I was a walking zombie and my consciousness was far from me. I barely felt Dante's assuring hands placed around my own. I only felt the cold of death as it tapped its vicious claws on my heart, reminding me that it was there and that I could do nothing to stop it.

Dante must've heard the cry escape from my mouth because he pulled me closer to him, forcing all of the darkness back into the corners of my heart.

"You okay?" he asked, caressing my shoulders. I shook my head in response. "Want anything to drink?" I shook my head again as I saw Norma burst into the waiting room. She took one nonchalant look at us before walking over to the nurse's desk to demand answers.

The doctor came out into the lobby and headed to Norma, who was still chastising the nurse for her ignorance. Dante guided me to where they stood, talking, and we both listened.

"What is the prognosis?" Norma asked the doctor. Worry lines formed on her forehead.

"We're still running tests, but it looks to be cancer related," the doctor somberly stated. "We noticed a lump on her leg. It could be a tumor. A lump that big could block off blood from getting to the brain, which could've resulted in her fainting. But these are only theories. We need to keep her for a few days."

"Can you operate on her leg?"

"Mrs. May is an older woman, and with a lump that size an operation would be detrimental to her health. If, say, the lump we found is cancerous, surgery could also increase the risk of the cancer spreading. I've seen cases like these where the leg needed to be amputated, however, that was for a much younger patient."

"Okay, so what if it is cancerous and you won't do surgery? What would be the next step?" Norma asked.

"I'd prefer to wait to discuss that further once we know for sure what the diagnosis is."

"Okay, how soon will you know?"

"Perhaps a couple more days," he said. "And I'm sorry, but visitation is prohibited at this point. You will need to wait to see her tomorrow."

"Why?" I asked.

The doctor looked at me for the first time. "She is in critical condition. Her heart gave out on her twice due to the blood being cut off from traveling to her heart. We need you to wait patiently until we decide what steps to take."

"When were you going to tell us that?" I asked, fuming.

"Will you call us when you have any update?" Norma asked, ignoring my question. The doctor seemed content to ignore it too.

"As soon as we have information, you will be updated."

Turned out, Momma May, in fact, did have a tumor the size of a baseball on her leg. The dresses she wore hid it well. I was shocked to learn that she kept it from us. I didn't understand why a woman of God would be deceiving. Dante said it was probably because she wanted to spare us the pain of knowing how much pain she was in. Momma May was never the type to complain, which made it hard to know when she was suffering.

I hated knowing that she suffered.

I spent the next few days making sure everything was perfect for her when she came home. I was praying it would be in a few more days. But it wasn't.

The doctor said they needed to keep her in the hospital longer. They had multiple specialists looking into ways to remove the tumor from her leg, and so far they were unsuccessful.

I really began to take my prayers seriously. I began spending more time reading the Bible firsthand, praying to understand how God works. Praying that He'd heal Momma May the way Jesus healed the blind. There was a story in the Bible where Jesus healed a man by saying, "You are forgiven." I took that as meaning it was the man's sin that made him sick and the forgiveness of that sin was what healed him. Maybe Momma May needed to be forgiven for something.

I could've been wrong. I never really understood how God worked.

Two dreadful weeks passed by slowly, a sad song on repeat. Every night I dreamt of sitting in an old, dark room as an old phonograph played in the corner. I wished to move, to turn the formidable music off, and to open the curtains so that sunlight would shine through. But the phonograph never cut off; it only collected more dust as I stayed trapped.

They say dreams are your subconscious thoughts. If that was true, I must've felt trapped in real life. In a sense, I was. There was nothing I could do to help out Momma May. I was helpless and afraid. I felt like every day was a dark day where no sunshine dared to intrude.

Just when I thought life couldn't get any worse, it did. And just when I found a woman who cared about me, one who helped me find Jesus, the one who took me in and became my momma, the one who constantly helped me try to get passed my own past, this happened. I was back at square one. But was I? If Momma May passed away, at least I could say I grew as a person. I could say I once knew the most beautiful woman God ever made.

But I couldn't stop wondering what would happen to me if she did pass away. Where would I go? How would I manage? Would I go back to my old ways of being fast and angry at the world? I hadn't really noticed the subtle changes I'd made in myself. Like the fact that I no longer felt the urge to act on impulse, doing crazy things like the time I stole Faith's dress. I didn't have a need to be the center of attention and that was because I felt loved. Yes, I made a pass at Dante, but only because my defenses were weakened. I was hurting and I needed some kind of affection. Dante happened to be the one who was there.

I wondered how Dante would manage if Momma May passed away. He'd known her much longer than I had. He was attached to her. I knew he'd take it harder than me. I could only imagine the thoughts that ran through his head when he learned about the tumor in Momma May's leg. He seemed quieter, on the edge, a fragile glass on the verge of cracking. But he held it together; he stayed strong for the both of us.

He came to the house every day at the same time and we played checkers, the way he and Momma May did. And then we'd go inside and watch TV, usually Momma May's favorite soaps. I'd cook and we'd busy ourselves with things to keep us sane. The routine helped; we needed the normalcy with all the chaos around.

Momma May finally was stable enough for us to visit. Dante drove us up there one day. I allowed him to visit her first while I sat in the waiting room, watching a couple get news of a death in the family from the doctor.

It was almost as if it was in slow motion. The doctor came from behind a door with a morose expression on his face. The couple jumped up, holding each other's hands with begging, desperate eyes. I couldn't make out what the doctor was telling them but I knew it was bad. The woman fell back into the man; his arms closed around her as he lowered his head. The woman's eyes stayed planted on the doctor as she cried.

"My baby!" she screamed. "My baby!"

I couldn't take it anymore. I stood up and left the waiting room. I didn't pay attention to where I walked. I just noticed families leaving hospital rooms as the nurses passed as they rushed along. I hoped they never had to go through what the couple earlier went through. I wouldn't wish that on anyone, not even John or Momma.

What if that would soon be Dante and me crying over the unfortunate news that Momma May passed away? I shook the thought out of my head.

I found my way back to the waiting room just as Dante was taking a seat. He stood up when he saw me. "She's awake. See her. It's room 306."

I nodded in relief. I hadn't realized how shaken up I was from seeing that couple lose someone close, a baby. I knew the feeling; I'd lost my own. I'd lost everything and yet was given more. It reminded me of the story of Job, who in the Bible lost everything: his house, his riches, and his family. But God gave everything back to Job tenfold. God is always faithful.

I was beginning to understand how He worked in my own life.

When I entered room 306 Momma May was barely conscious, but her eyes lit up once she heard me. My heart warmed, forgetting all of the negative things that weighed it down. I ran to her side and kissed her cheek. I ran a hand through her beautiful silver-white hair the way I always did. I loved brushing the curls and watching them spring up as if I'd never straightened them. A tear escaped my eye and I watched as Momma May struggled to lift her hand.

"Why are you crying, child?"

I loved her sweet Southern accent, much stronger than my own. "I missed you."

"Wipe those tears and rejoice. It's what Jesus would say. Rejoice for having another day with me. Rejoice."

I smiled. "That's why I'm crying. It's happy tears."

She nodded. "You been keeping my house up?"

"Yes, ma'am."

"Dante said so. God has been good to me bringing that boy into my life." She coughed. "He's making sure everyone is doing their job at the church, called in pastors to preach in my spot. I've had so many phone calls from my members praying over me. I'm sure they'd be up here if I could have visitors besides family. Heck, they are my family." Momma May laughed. Her voice was croaky. "And I am truly blessed to have you, Hope. I appreciate you keeping my house in order."

"No, I appreciate you. I owe you that much, Momma May."

She smiled. "You're turning into a fine young woman, Hope. Everything about you is growing, do you see it?"

I hadn't really thought about it.

Momma May continued. "You're growing spiritually and emotionally. God has been blessing you abundantly. For a girl to come out of the life you did and grow into a fine young woman is a blessing. Hope, I want to see you continue to grow. Get back in to high school, go to college, make something out of your life."

"School." I hadn't been in so long.

"What do you want to be in life, Hope?"

I hadn't really thought about it. I spent most of my time thinking about the past, never the future. I didn't have any real talents besides singing. I had no skills, I was an average student, and I had no passion for anything.

"I don't know."

"Well, you need to start thinking about it."

"Is it because you think you're gonna die?"

Momma May's hands found mine as I studied her face. She had lost a lot of color. Her face had sunken in, and her body looked fragile under the white covers.

"I'm not thinking about myself, only you and your well-being, Hope. I took you in and promised myself and God that I'd help you grow. I will fulfill that promise. I will serve the Lord, even on my deathbed."

"Don't say that!" I said, tears rushing down my face. "You ain't on your deathbed!"

Momma May didn't say anything for a long time but when she spoke, her voice commanded the whole room. If my eyes were closed, I would have thought it was a much younger, powerful woman.

"We must always obey the Lord, even when He calls us home. I am not saying it is my time, but when it is, I will go serving the Lord," she said.

I didn't want to talk about her dying so I changed the subject to something I could handle. "What they gonna do about your leg?"

"There ain't nothing they can do."

"So they just gonna let the cancer spread?" I felt my heart drop.

"It's already spread everywhere."

I stood at the side of her bed, helpless and angry. I didn't have the power to cure Momma May. There was absolutely nothing I could do to help her. I prayed every night and grew closer to the Lord, hoping He'd cure

Momma May. She was mine. He gave us to each other. Why would He tear us apart so soon?

I couldn't contain my anger any longer and ran out of the room, brushing passed nurses until I emerged into the waiting room where Dante sat. He looked up at me but I said nothing. I ran straight past him to the elevators, franticly pressing the arrow button. I looked up at the number at the top of the elevator and noticed it was on floor thirteen, ten floors above.

I felt Dante's presence as he approached, but I ignored the urge to turn to him. I wanted to be left alone. I also didn't want to take my anger out on him. Who knew that when I watched that woman mourn for the loss of her child I'd be feeling a similar pain today? Strange how we all connect through pain and joy. It's two of the things all humans share.

"Hope."

I ignored him. The elevator had reached the sixth floor. I tapped my foot impatiently, needing to break out of the hospital, needing air. I felt claustrophobic and tried every technique possible to keep myself from freaking out. The elevator door finally opened and I rushed inside. Dante followed.

I pressed the button and kept my eyes ahead, trying hard not the blink in fear of the tears that were almost tipping over my eyelids. As soon as the door opened, I tried to rush out but Dante grabbed my hand, pulling me back in. He quickly hit a button on the panel that caused the elevator door to close and shut down. He then turned me around to face him and pulled me close, pressing his lips to mine. At first I was shocked and tried to push him away but that didn't last long. Soon, I joined in the kiss, wrapping my arms around him, lifting up on my tippy toes to be even with him.

When the kiss ended, I couldn't speak. Tears streamed freely but Dante kissed them away.

"Shh," he said, his voice instantly calming me. I didn't know what came over us. What changed. It was him, the way he looked at me, with passion, with clarity. "Don't cry."

"Dante, you just sinned."

He smiled, his forehead touching mine. "You'll be my wife one day. It was worth it."

I backed away, flabbergasted. "What?"

"Pastor May prophesied it to me today. She told me that God came to her in a dream and showed her our future. She said we'd get married and that I needed to protect you." His eyes grew dark as he looked down. "She told me that she won't be here much longer and that the devil is working hard to destroy you. I have to be your strength and I want to."

"Is that why you kissed me?"

"You needed it. You need affection and love."

I blinked a few times, trying to wake up from this dream: one where Dante was strong and sure of himself, a quality he hadn't possessed until now. Or maybe I just hadn't noticed it. But I didn't awaken from a dream. Dante was still in front of me, looking at me. He seemed almost happy. But how could he be happy? Momma May practically told him that she'd die soon. It was just like Momma May to be selfless and think of us when she knew she'd pass away.

The thought angered me again.

Dante pressed the button and the door opened. He grabbed my hand and led me out of the elevator. Once we were in his car, he began questioning me. "Why did you run out of the hospital like that?"

I sighed, not wanting to recall the horror of finding out Momma May would die. But I needed to talk to someone about it. I couldn't keep holding my pain inside.

"I ran out because she pretty much said she'd die soon, and I couldn't handle it. Dante, why?" I started crying. "Why is God doing this? Why does He always take people out of my life? I thought I was like Job! I thought I was gonna be blessed with more than what I lost but I just keep losing."

He shook his head. "No, you're not. You're winning. We aren't meant to understand why God operates the way He does. You've gained everything."

"Momma May is my everything and if He takes her . . ." I couldn't even finish the sentence.

"It wasn't Momma May God blessed you with, it was her love, knowledge, and wisdom that He gave you. But when she passes, He'll give you the love of another. Me."

"I just don't wanna lose her," I said, fighting back a round of tears.

"You're not losing anything. One day, you'll be in heaven with her. We are to keep our eyes on the Kingdom."

"It's easier said than done when you can't even see the Kingdom. I can't help but to keep my eyes on what's around me. It's easier for Momma May because she can't see!"

"That's not true. If you were blind, you'd focus so much more on what's around you because you can't see it. You may bump into things, so you have to use all of your senses to get around it. That should've taken up her mind alone but, no, she focused even more on God and the Kingdom. She has peace."

"Peace? No, Dante. She looked almost dead. She said the cancer spread all through her body! What am I gonna do if she dies? Where am I gonna go?"

"With me." He said it so simply. I almost forgot about what he told me on the elevator about how we'd get married. I was too consumed by my own pain to think about it.

Was it true? Did God really talk to Momma May in her dreams? I'd heard of such things but never experienced it firsthand. Did I even want to marry Dante, the person who annoyed me the most? Well, he also made me laugh, helped me, and had been my right-hand man. We'd kissed, twice. Slept in the same bed (Jesus forgive me). Argued and made up. He was just as much a part of me as Momma May. I'd taken him for granted. But that didn't mean I wanted to marry him!

I looked over at his troubled expression as he drove. The radio played gospel songs in the background. I looked out of my window at the clouds, which gloomed ominously above, threatening to rain down on what I had left. I decided in that moment, I wouldn't let anyone take Dante from me, even God. He was mine, now. One day soon, he'd be the only thing I had left.

Chapter 17

It's a weird feeling when the Holy Spirit places conviction on the heart. I woke up in the middle of the night in a sweat. I was disoriented, not fully understanding where I was. But reality sank in quickly. I remembered the hospital visit with Momma May and Dante telling me about the prophecy. But something else had been bothering me.

"Lord Jesus," I said, and then it hit me.

My relationship with John. What I did was malicious, revolting, and classless. I seduced John and he wasn't just any man. He was my mom's boyfriend. She loved him and I ruined it. Not to mention how John could've gone to jail for his relationship with me. I was ashamed.

"God, please forgive me!" I cried. "Please forgive me of all of the things I did not only to Momma but to Faith."

In that moment, I understood what Momma May meant when she said I'd grown spiritually. If someone would've asked me months ago how I felt about how I ruined my mother's relationship with John, I would've laughed and said I'd do it again in a heartbeat. But God had been working on me silently ever since I welcomed Him into my heart. He had opened up my mind, especially within the last two weeks. He'd drawn me closer to Him.

But I still didn't want to go to church. I just couldn't fathom it. It was a demon I was still battling.

Dante and I headed back to the hospital that next day. I was afraid I had offended Momma May the way I ran out of her room the day before. I hoped she understood.

I stood outside of her door, composing myself, steadying my breathing. I wanted to be strong for her.

I opened the door and stepped inside. She was leaning against the bed, which was bent upward so that she could listen to her soaps. Flowers and teddy bears and balloons decorated the stand in the room. Another person was seated in the chair next to the bed. It was a woman a little younger than Momma May, with graying hair and a sweet smile.

"This must be Hope," the woman said. "I'm Joyce."

"Hi," I said, walking into the room. I looked at Momma May, who seemed in good spirits.

"May told me all about you and I'm glad to finally meet you." Joyce turned to Momma May and squeezed her hand. "I got to head up to the church and handle things. Everybody at the church has been praying."

"Yeah, they've called and came to visit. Tell everyone that I am doing good and can't wait to get back to church," Momma May said. Joyce squeezed her hand again and stood to leave. She smiled as she walked passed me.

"Take care of her," she said and left the room.

I took a seat beside Momma May. Although she seemed happy, she hadn't improved at all. Her eyes were sinking in and she barely had any meat on her bones. At least her silver hair lay intact. I had brought her favorite brush from home, knowing she would love for me to brush her hair with it. I pulled it from my purse and began brushing her soft hair. She smiled, eating the candy Dante brought her.

"Boston Baked Beans, my favorite," she said, chewing on the candy. "And I love when you brush my hair."

"I love to brush it."

"Baby, come around on the other side of the bed and look in the closet. There is a bag. I had Norma bring it up here earlier."

I set the brush down next to her and did as she said. A large white bag hung in the little closet. It was the kind of bag that I remembered all too well. The type of bag Momma used to bring home for Faith. I grabbed the bag and shut the door.

"Open it."

I smiled, feeling my heart putter in my chest. I unzipped the bag and pulled out a beautiful short-sleeved vintage off-white dress that ruffled on the arms and flowed to the ground. It was a simple dress with not much design, but that didn't matter. It was the style of the dress that was stunning, like something I pictured a flapper in the twenties getting married in.

And then I realized what kind of a dress it was.

"I married in that dress." Momma May smiled. "I know I'm always telling the same stories. I'm an old lady." Her laugh caused her to go into a coughing fit. "Remember the day I told you about not being able to fit in my old wedding dress? Well, that was before I got this dress. I remember the day like it was yesterday. I was about your size when I was pregnant and got married. After a few alterations to the waistline, it should fit you perfectly."

"You want me to get married in it?" I asked, not able to hide the surprise in my voice.

She laughed. "If you choose to, one day, but I just want you to have it. I've been holding on to it, never wanting to give it up. My kids tried to convince me to but I couldn't, especially after my husband died. But I decided to give it to you. If anyone would appreciate a dress, it would be you."

I held the dress up to my body, picturing myself in it. I laughed out loud; I couldn't contain the joy. I spun around with the dress in my hand, remembering how Faith used to twirl around whenever she got a pretty dress. It was the best feeling.

"This is the best gift. Thank you." I put the dress back in the bag and sat on the edge of her bed. "I'm sorry for running out yesterday. I just—"

"It's okay, Hope. I understand."

I nodded and began fiddling with my fingers. "Dante told me about the prophecy."

She smiled. "I know he did."

I nodded again. "Do you think you'll live to see that day happen? You know, when we get . . . married?" It was so hard to say those words, especially because I hadn't grown accustomed to them.

"Only the good Lord knows."

"How long do you have to live?" I asked.

"The doctors don't want to put a time stamp on it. They said it could be months or it could be weeks."

I bent over, feeling pain course through my stomach, and tried to fight the urge to cry. I waited until my breathing was steady to speak again. "I pray every night for God to heal you."

"I lived a long life. When God takes me, I'll go gladly. But don't worry about me, baby. Worry about the life you still have left. "

"Everything is happening too fast. Two weeks ago you were fine. I didn't even think about the cancer. I thought you was gonna be fine. And then you passed out and they found that tumor. Why didn't you tell us about the tumor?"

"I didn't want to scare you."

"Maybe they could've helped you get better if they caught it early!"

"It grew bigger in the course of a week. There was nothing they would have been able to do. I had a doctor's appointment scheduled to get it checked out but then I ended up in the hospital. I would've told all of you once I knew what was wrong," she told me.

"I know you're probably tired of talking about it," I said, but I was talking more to myself. I didn't want to keep hearing about the negatives. It was consuming my thoughts. I needed a break from life. I wanted to hear about times where Momma May was truly happy in life. Maybe that would dissipate the tension and pain in the air. I lay down beside her on the bed. "Tell me stories about your life . . . the good ones."

She smiled.

"My life is full of good stories, baby. But since I gave you my wedding dress, I'll tell you more about my wedding day," she started. "Back then, when my husband was just founding his church, we barely had two pennies to rub together. We didn't know what we would eat most days. Our house, same one I live in today, barely held the rain out. All of his money went into the church. We had to rely solely on God and His promise to always provide. And He did. Everybody in our town loved my husband and donated things to make our wedding special. His mother's friend worked for a rich woman who had a garden and was able to get those flowers to make me a bouquet. Others made food and drinks for the ceremony. One man worked at a hall and was able to reserve it for our wedding day. Everything was great. I just didn't have a wedding dress.

"One day I woke up and found a beautiful dress lying neatly on my porch. It had no note. Nothing. I went around town asking everyone who gave me the dress but nobody knew. Nobody had the kind of money to buy that dress. It was the kind we saw white women wear, an expensive one. And here it was, just sitting on my porch, brand new and glorious. My husband said it was a gift from God and that there was no other explanation for it. To this day, I still truly believe one of God's angels set that dress on my porch. That's why I kept it so close to me like I keep all of God's gifts."

"And now you're giving it to me." I smiled. "I love it even more."

I spent a couple more hours in the hospital talking and laughing with Momma May. It was interesting how some of my deepest moments together happened when she was in the hospital. I lived in a world where tragedy and sadness brought people together.

I lay in bed that night, picturing a God who cared for me as much as He cared for Momma May. She was an amazing woman, like David, after God's own heart. She preached the gospel, even in old age, and was honest when she said she'd serve the Lord until death. I didn't even know such women existed. I was so used to women like Momma, who did not know God. Maybe if she had, she would've been a better person. It wasn't too late. Even I knew that God could still save her.

The thought gave me an idea.

That next day I asked Dante to drive me out to my old house. I made sure I went around the time Momma got off of work. I knew that Faith would be there and I needed to see her, too. I wanted to apologize for my actions that separated us and caused all of our problems. I wanted to share the gospel with Momma in hopes that she'd come to God. I was at a point where I wanted to forgive. I needed to. I'd die of a heart attack due to the amount stress on my heart. And if God could forgive me, I should forgive others.

It took almost an hour before we pulled up on the gravel road that led to the house. Everything was as I remembered it: a small, ugly house in the middle of many acres that didn't belong to us. I noticed the tree in the front still had my tire swing. I remember kissing John there, our first kiss.

Too many bad memories.

Dante sat beside me, taking everything in with a curious expression. "So this is where you used to live."

"I wasn't living when I stayed here." I wasn't sure if he understood what I meant, but he nodded.

"Are you ready?"

"No," I said, but I got out of the car anyway.

Dante followed as I approached the door. I didn't even make it to the front step before Faith stepped out on the porch. She looked the same and was wearing a beautiful dress with a nice bun in her hair. The sight made my eyes water. I expected her to run down the stairs and straight into my arms, but she didn't. She was still angry with me.

"Hope," was all she said.

"Faith," I began, but didn't know what to say. I decided to go with an introduction. "This is Dante," I said. And to Dante, I said, "This is Faith, my twin."

"Nice to finally meet you," Dante said.

Faith's eyes glanced uneasily between the two of us. "Is this who you was staying with?"

"Naw, I'm staying with . . ." But I wasn't able to finish. From the corner of my eyes, I saw Momma slowly step out onto the porch. She folded her arms and stood in place. I'd never seen her react so quietly. I was almost filled with joy. I thought she may have forgiven me, but then I remembered the saying, "the calm before the storm."

I walked away from Dante and stood at the bottom step, looking up at Momma, whose face was stoic and impassive. I sighed, running through the things I wanted to say to her and I decided to start with an apology.

Momma smirked. "You sorry? You came all the way out here to tell me you sorry? You think I believe that?" She started walking down the steps toward me. She seemed to have aged since the last time I saw her.

"Yes, you should," I told her. "I gave my life to Jesus and He says we should forgive those who sinned against us and to seek forgiveness from those we've sinned against."

She laughed out loud. "You think God wants you? You want me to believe it was God who brought you here? Not the devil? 'Cause the devil been wrapped around you since you was a little girl. Ain't no hope in you. I don't even know why I named you that."

Her venomous words entered my bloodstream, choosing first to attack my heart. I wanted to collapse, break my strong resolve under her stare, but God tugged at my heart and pulled my shoulders back. When my own strength failed me, He replaced it with His.

"I am not the devil and he don't control me. I came here to ask for forgiveness and to tell you to seek forgiveness in your own sins and turn to Jesus. There is a God who is greater than all of our problems. He's changing me every day, making me stronger, allowing me to understand my own errors so that I can correct them. That's what I'm trying to do now, Momma. I'm trying to get my life together in every way, but I can't move forward until I forgive my past and be forgiven of it."

Momma stared at me for a while, not saying anything. She looked as if she was touched. "That was a nice speech," she said, but then her lips turned into a wicked smile. "Faith, wasn't that nice and believable? Something one of the Christian folk at your church would say?" She looked down at me. "Do they say those things at your church, Hope? Huh?"

I lowered my head, understanding where she was taking the conversation. Church. She knew how wounded I was from never being given the chance to go. How I took my anger out on God. How I hated churches. If I was a true Christian, I should've been able to get passed that.

But I hadn't. Every time I thought about going to church, I pictured the little girl who sat under the peach tree, singing those songs, and wondering why God or her family didn't love her. I associated church with neglect.

I wasn't passed it, but I was getting better. However, to Momma, it still wouldn't be good enough. I'd never be good enough for her.

"So, how's church, Hope?" she asked, snapping me out of my reverie.

My palms were sweaty; I felt my resolve threaten to shatter. I took a step forward, feeling lower than I had felt before she began antagonizing me. But it was Dante who spoke. He walked past me, meeting Momma's burning eyes with his quiet confidence.

"Church. It's funny you mentioned it. Which church do you attend?" he asked Momma.

Momma was dumbfounded. "I don't go to church."

"Hypocrite?" he asked, but it was more accusing than anything. "The Bible says, 'How can you say to your brother, "Brother, let me take the speck out of your eye," when you yourself fail to see the plank in your own eye? You hypocrite, first take the plank out of your eye, and then you will see clearly to remove the speck from your brother's eye.' Luke 6:42. Do you know what that means?"

Momma stood there, insecure under Dante's gaze. I'd never noticed the amount of influence Dante had over people. I'd never realized his strength until now. Faith even watched Dante with admiration. "What does that mean?" Momma asked.

"It means don't degrade another for the same faults you have. Fix your errors and then correct theirs. I've never met someone as beautiful and blessed as Hope, and she doesn't see her own worth because her mother told her that she'd never be anything good. I brought her all the way out here to seek forgiveness and to share the Lord with you, but how can she when you're so bent on holding on to the past? Maybe it was a mistake bringing her out here, but we'll continue to pray that God softens your heart. We'll also pray for your salvation." Dante turned around to me. "Let's go."

He started walking away but I stayed, planted to the ground. I wasn't done. There was something I needed to say, something that had been burdening me. Momma needed to know.

I stepped closer to my mother, the woman who gave birth to me. The only person whose love I would've cherished more than anything. To hear her say she loved me would've been the best thing in the world, but I knew it wouldn't happen today. Instead, I'd show her how much I'd grown, how far I'd come.

"I'm sorry for what I did with John. I'm sorry I ruined your relationship. I'm sorry I was never as good as Faith in your eyes. I'm sorry I failed you so many times. And for all the times you've never said it to me, I'll say it to you and mean it from the bottom of my heart. I love you. I love you. I love you. I love you. I love you."

I thought I saw a moment of passion in Momma's eyes, a moment of clarity, one that would mean we'd just reached a milestone, but as quickly as it had come, it vanished, and her eyes were as hard as stone. She looked at me as if I was a piece of trash.

"Get her off of my property!"

Dante grabbed me, pulling me away from the house, but my eyes never left Momma. They pleaded with her to forgive me, to say those three words back to me, but they never came out of her mouth. Dante sat me in the car and buckled my seat belt. He had been talking to me, but I tuned him out. My eyes stayed locked on Momma, who still stood on the porch, staring at me even when Faith had gone back inside. A part of me wanted to believe she still stood there because she loved me. I wanted to believe it; I needed to. As we drove off, and I kept mumbling the same words over and over until I fell asleep from exhaustion.

"Momma, I love you."

I meant it, even if she never would.

Chapter 18

I stood beside Momma May's hospital bed, brushing her silver hair the way I did every morning when Dante and I came to visit. She loved that part, being pampered. I'd also massaged the bottom of her legs and feet and propped them up on a pillow so that the circulation would be better. She wasn't able to walk around as much since she'd been in the hospital, so I promised myself that I'd put her at ease whenever I visited. Besides, I didn't know how much longer I'd have with her.

She was already starting to look thinner, weaker, worse than the last time I'd seen her. Her hands were nothing but bones and skin. The lump on her leg grew larger and could be seen from under her covers. I'd noticed how her eyes squinted shut whenever she was in pain, and that happened often, but she never complained. Not once.

All she did was thank God.

"Oh, God is good, isn't He?" she said, as I began to massage her feet.

I looked up at her. "How can you say that when you're in so much pain?"

"Long suffering. Waiting patiently for the Lord to bring me home. I'll take the pain because the worse it gets, the closer I get to finally seeing Jesus' face. And in that, I am thankful."

"How are you so faithful in Jesus? How can you be happy and praise Him even when you're in pain?" I asked. I didn't understand. If I was in pain, I'd probably be angry with God, not happy. As a matter of fact, that's how I'd spent most of my life, in pain, hating God.

"Baby, it's something that takes awhile to master, to fully understand. You're young, Hope. Still a baby in Christ. It'll take knowledge and experience and fasting and prayer to understand God the way that I do. But you'll get there. I have faith in that," she said, closing her eyes. I knew the pain was hitting her.

Could I ever praise God through my pain? Could I ever understand the way she did? I made sure to make a mental note to pray about it.

"You never did tell me how it made you feel to forgive your momma, Hope."

The first thing I did, as I began brushing her hair, was tell her about my trip to Momma's house. Momma May was very proud of me and said that it was Jesus working through me and that I wouldn't have been able to forgive Momma by myself. I wasn't sure if I even truly forgave her, but it was a start.

"I felt a weight lifted off of my shoulders but I also felt sad because she never said she loved me back."

"She will. One day, Hope. God works on us all in His own time. She's a little slower than some of us, but God will get her there. It may take months, even years, but keep faith in knowing that the Lord will show her the errors in her ways. He will fill her heart with compassion toward you. You two will be able to hold hands and walk into a church together, praising God. Together."

I smiled. "I doubt it, but I'll pray about it."

"You do that."

That next day, Momma May beat the side effect of her medicine, which caused drowsiness, and was able to stay awake long enough to tell me stories about her childhood. I always loved those moments: being able to see into her life. I was able to see how God used her, even when she hadn't realized He was doing anything. I got to see how God took her problems and brought nothing but good from them.

"I never really had a mother because she died when I was young," Momma May began. "My grandma raised me on nothing but strict discipline and the Bible. I wasn't allowed to go outside and play with the neighborhood kids. I had to come straight home from school and study the Bible. She punished me by making me learn Bible verse after verse and, afterward, writing paragraphs on what those verses meant.

"I got to the point where I hated the Bible and God. I thought He was just like my grandmother, all sternness and no fun. Always watching, waiting for me to mess up so that He could scold me, like my grandmother. I was a lot like you, Hope. I ran away from God because my grandmother used Him as a means to break me. When I was sixteen, I ran away from my grandmother's house and found work with the mayor and his wife. I didn't find God again until I was blinded."

"Shouldn't that make you hate Him more?"

"You'd think, but at that point, I realized I needed Him more than anything. God had turned her harsh punishment into good. If my grandmother hadn't been so strict on me learning the Bible, I would've never been able to step into ministry the way I did. It was also another thing that attracted my husband to me. He prayed to God for a woman who knew His word like the back of her hand, to help Him to minister to the people. God gave him me. I was that woman.

"Do you understand the point of this story, Hope? God can take any bad thing and turn it into good to glorify Him. So whatever pain you go through that you don't understand, know that God is working something out, and one day, you'll be able to look back and understand why you went through so much. Your testimony will be great."

And I believed her. My testimony would one day change lives. Momma May was right; we were a lot alike.

Norma came over to the house that weekend, reeking of alcohol. Dante had made it a habit of staying the night and he made sure to sleep on the couch downstairs. If Momma May knew we were in that house alone, she'd kill us both. Dante made it apparent that we weren't to do anything disrespectful, and he followed through.

We were sitting on the couch, watching a movie we'd ordered, when Norma burst through the door, almost falling to the ground. She saw us sitting on the couch and stumbled over to us.

"What y'all doin' in this house un*sooo*pervised?" she slurred, sweat dripping from her forehead. She looked as if she'd run here. Her clothes were wrinkled and hanging off of her and her hair was falling shamelessly in her face. "Well since ya here, I gotta . . . ask ya a q . . . question."

"You're drunk," I said.

Norma gave me a disgusted look. "What would ya do if ya grandma was dyin'?" she asked me.

"Spend more time with her," I answered.

She shook her head and directed her attention on Dante. "I need some money," she barked. "Give me some money."

"You're drunk," he said, but at this point it was already obvious.

"Well, obviously I am, and what that gotta do with my money? I need some money. You gonna give it to me?"

"What do you need it for?" Dante asked.

"Why I gotta tell you?" Norma asked. "I need some money! Give me some money."

"If you want money, you're going to have to tell me why you need it, Norma," Dante firmly stated.

"It ain't none of your business why I need it! If you ain't gonna give it to me, I'll just take it from Momma's bank."

Norma clumsily turned toward the staircase and began climbing it. I looked at Dante, trying to figure out what money Norma was referring to. He jumped up, running upstairs after Norma. I jumped up, following, trying to figure out what was going on.

We found Norma in Momma May's room. She had removed a large picture from the wall and was trying to break the combination to the safe hidden inside the wall. She cursed when she couldn't open it.

"Pastor May had me change the password, Norma. She knew you'd been getting into her money when she had me sit down and count it all after she got out of the hospital the first time. Ten thousand dollars was missing, and that's not even including the thirty thousand dollar loan you took out on her property. She knows about that, too, because I told her. She also knows about your drug problem. I gotta admit you hid that one well, too."

I was completely surprised, not knowing Norma had a drug problem. I had noticed something slightly off about her but was never able to put my finger on it. Now I understood why she stayed gone a lot since I'd taken over helping Momma May. She hadn't brought the kids over in a while, either.

Norma screamed in frustration, running a shaky hand through her hair. "I know I got a problem, but I need that money. I need it, Dante! Give it to me." She ran over to him and tried checking his pockets. He gently pushed her away but she was persistent. "Give me the money!"

That was when I jumped between them, pushing Norma back. Her eyes blazed as she looked up from where she landed on the floor. "You little . . ." She tried to jump up, but fell back on the ground. She decided to lay there with her hands covering her face and she moaned.

I turned to Dante. "I didn't mean to make her fall but she was getting crazy."

"Thanks," he said. "Help me get her up. She needs to sober up before she overdoses on whatever she took."

"Ain't she just drunk?"

He shook his head. "She's been doing coke on and off for years. Looks like she's back on it now. Probably because of the stress of Momma May. It's good to have sharp eyes, Hope. I used to watch her take Momma May's mail but I didn't understand why and so I left it alone. Makes sense now, she was probably hiding delinquency letters. She probably took a lot of measures to keep Momma May from finding out. Come on, help me lift her and take her to the bathroom."

I walked over by her feet as Dante stood by her head. He lifted her by her shoulders, instructing me to grab her feet. Together we carried her into the bathroom and sat her in the tub.

"Undress her and run cold water over her. I'm going to get some ice water for her to drink," he said, and left the bathroom.

I struggled with getting her wet clothes off of her body, but I managed and covered her with a towel by the time Dante returned with the water.

"Lift her up," he said.

I looked down at Norma, who started shaking under the cold water while mumbling words between con-sciousness. I sat her back and tilted her head so that Dante could pour the water down her throat. At first she struggled and choked as we forced her to drink, but then she began to welcome it. Maybe it was her body telling her that she needed it. All along, I didn't stop praying for God to heal her sickness. I wouldn't wish addiction on any soul.

We stayed that way for a half hour, forcing her to drink water. Eventually she threw everything up and passed out in the tub. Dante and I carried her into my room and left her to sleep it off. I eventually crawled into Momma May's bed and fell asleep.

When I woke up the next day, Norma was already gone. I went downstairs and found Dante still asleep on the couch but he had changed his clothes since last night. He looked peaceful, like an angel. Maybe he was an angel in his own way.

If someone would've told me the day I first met the boy with no fashion sense or rhythm, who had freckles and a shy disposition, that I'd marry him, I would've died of laughter. But looking at him now, seeing how much he'd grown over the last few months, how fond I was of him, I could believe it. I loved him, in my own way. Looking down at him, with my heart beating wildly in my chest, I could guess I was beginning to fall in love with him.

Dante opened his eyes as if he'd sensed me watching him. He smiled sleepily. "Happy birthday!"

My mouth dropped open. With everything going on, I hadn't realized today was my seventeenth birthday. I'd grown accustomed to never really caring about that day, since Momma never did anything special for me and I didn't know how to feel about it now.

Dante sat up. "Did you forget today is your birthday?"

I nodded.

"Who forgets their own birthday? I know people who plan birthday parties months in advance."

"Well . . ." I sat next to him. "I never celebrated my birthday so it was always just another day where Faith got presents and I didn't."

He smiled. "Well, we have the rest of your life to make up for it. Get dressed, we have a big day ahead of us."

My eyes widened. "What? A big day? How?"

He stood up, stretching. "Don't ask questions, just go get dressed."

Turned out, Dante had woken up at five in the morning, got dressed, and let Norma out. He said she was sober when she woke up and barely said a word due to embarrassment. He then got dressed, lay back on the couch, and slept until I woke up.

We started our day off as normal. We went up to the hospital. Dante played checkers with Momma May, as usual, and I waited until it was my turn to go back and see her. We preferred to have our individual space with her, but some days we'd visit her together. When I arrived, Momma May had a box, wrapped up in beautiful paper, sitting on the table.

"Happy birthday, baby," she said.

"Thanks." I felt joy at knowing people actually cared about my birthday.

"There is a box on that stand. I had Dante do some shopping for me. Go on and open it."

I sat down in the chair beside the bed, holding the gift in my hand. I almost felt undeserving to receive the gift. I could hear Momma in my head telling me that I'd probably done something and shouldn't deserve it. I ran through the most recent actions and events in my life, trying to find a reason to feel bad. It was natural for me. I didn't know how to feel anything but.

I started unwrapping the silver wrapping paper until I was left with a white box. I slowly opened it, cherishing each moment.

A beautiful pair of earrings shimmered inside. They looked like diamonds, but I knew better than to believe Momma May would spend that much money on a pair of diamonds.

"They're beautiful."

"They're real diamonds," she said. "Every girl deserves a nice pair of diamond earrings. I remembered when my husband bought me my first pair. I wore them for three weeks straight. Dante picked them out, does he have good taste?"

"More than good," I said, eyes watering. I didn't know how she could afford diamond earrings. "I don't deserve this much love."

"Yes, you do, baby. Yes, you do," she said. "Now don't cry on your birthday, be happy. Thank God you've lived to see one better than anything you could've imagined. Thank God, baby."

I smiled, and thanked God. I thanked Him for the new life He'd blessed me with. The friend I found in Dante, the mother I found in May, the woman I found inside of myself. That little girl was growing up. Happy birthday to me.

Chapter 19

Dante wouldn't tell me what he had planned for my birthday. He just drove with a smile on his face and said nothing whenever I asked . . . and I asked every few minutes. He pulled up in front of Rising Faith Ministries and turned off the car. I frowned, wondering why we were even at the church.

"Your gift is inside. Come on." Dante opened the car door.

"Inside of the church?" My words came out as a whisper. Sweat began to drip from my forehead. I was frozen in my seat.

"Yes, come on."

"No!" I yelled a little too loudly. "I'm not going in there!"

Dante sighed. "You got to get past your fears if you want the gift."

"How about you bring it to me? Because I ain't going in there."

"You have to come inside to get it, Hope. You can do it."

"No, Dante, you don't understand." I sighed in frustration. "I'm not ready to step foot into a church. I can't do it."

"Hope, you're never going to be ready. You have to face your fears head-on. You can do it."

Tears started pouring from my eyes as I shook my head. "No, why would you do this? You can't force someone to get over their fears, Dante. I'm not going in that church.

I'm not. Forget the gift. I don't care! This is the worst birthday. Just take me home!" I yelled, causing Dante to look hurt.

"After everything I did to prepare for this, after everything Pastor May did, you say this is your worst birthday?" He was truly hurt. He shut his car door and started the car. "Pastor May must be wrong about that dream she had about us getting married. I wouldn't marry a selfish girl who says she loves God but can't step foot into His house."

"Why would you say that?"

"Because it's the truth!" Dante sped off, knocking me back in my seat. I'd never seen him angry before. He was full of surprises.

I did feel bad about my comment, stating it was the worst birthday. That wasn't true. It was the best birthday but just one of my worst moments. I almost had a panic attack and Dante didn't understand.

If I was selfish, so was he. You couldn't force someone to do something they didn't want to do, especially on their birthday, and then get mad at them. He cared more about me going in to that church than the actual gift he would give me.

Dante dropped me off without saying a word, and kept on going. I was hurt that he wouldn't stay the night, the way he had every day since Momma May had been in the hospital. I felt empty and alone in that house. I went straight to my room and slept the rest of my birthday evening away.

That next day, Dante didn't show up to take me to the hospital the way he did every morning. I called up to the hospital and spoke with Momma May, who said Dante was sitting at the edge of her bed playing checkers. I almost hung up on Momma May in anger. After I got off of the phone with her, I decided to catch the bus just to show Dante that I didn't need him or his car.

By the time I got to the hospital, Dante was already gone. Momma May was in a deep sleep and I decided not to wake her. So I just sat there, reliving the past few days and allowing everything to sink in.

I thought about Norma's drug problem and how she was able to hide it so well. When I first met her, I thought she was a beautiful, light-skinned woman, with beautiful silky hair, much like Faith's. She looked like she had a great job and a beautiful family. But now, I wasn't so sure. It could've all been a façade. I prayed that her kids weren't affected by her drug addiction.

And then I thought about how angry Dante was with me. Out of all people, he and Momma May seemed to be the most understanding. How could he have thought he'd be able to convince me to go into that church? No present on earth was enough to convince me to go inside of a church. It only reminded me of a childhood I wished to forget. It only made me feel empty and unloved. I didn't want that. I didn't want to relive any of it. Maybe Momma was right; maybe I really didn't belong to God if I wouldn't even step foot into a church.

But the fact that Dante acted so unchristian-like was what bothered me. He was the strong one, rooted firmly in the Word. Surely there was a scripture in the Bible preaching against how he behaved. Maybe Proverbs? I hadn't really gotten into Proverbs yet, but I heard it was a book that taught wisdom and knowledge. But Dante held on to his anger. He said hurtful things to me. He went to see Momma May without me. I was so angry, I couldn't care less whether he ever spoke to me again.

But if he never did and if Momma May died who would I have? God. I knew I'd have God. But that was different from having an actual human near. Even God Himself said that it wasn't good for man to be alone. I wasn't the type of girl who liked solitude. It was in the quiet of nights that the devil burdened my thoughts with insecurities. He whispered them so subtly that I thought they were my own thoughts. I didn't like to be alone, let alone cry over the things I couldn't change.

Dread entered my heart, a dark, abysmal feeling that suffocated me. I inhaled sharply, holding my chest, trying not to cry. Momma May was going to pass away soon. I couldn't fathom it.

"Hope?" Momma May's blind eyes searched the room until she heard me inhale again. "When did you get here, baby?"

"Maybe ten minutes ago. How you feeling today?"

"Blessed. Dante told me what happened."

"I hate him," I said in anger.

"Hate is a strong word, baby. You should say that you 'dislike' his actions at the moment."

"I dislike his actions, period. I can't stand him, Momma May."

"Ah, there were times where I couldn't stand my own husband." She laughed, recalling a memory. "I remember when we had our first big argument. We'd just been married for a week. We'd moved everything into our new house and was settled for the most part. But what he didn't understand was that I was blind in a new home. I couldn't easily feel my way around the house like I usually could. It would take weeks to get familiar enough with that house before I could comfortably walk around. So he had to do everything, plus work and minister on Sundays. I felt really bad about my handicap. But he never complained. I thought it was because he understood. But, baby, men don't always understand how we operate. See, he had been holding his irritation in that eventually it exploded and I was the one in its path."

"What happened?"

"I asked him to get me something to drink and he said, 'You got two legs, get your own drink! I'm tired of catering to your every need! You better feel your way into that kitchen, woman!'"

My eyes widened. "He said that?"

"Oh yes, he did. And he didn't stop there either. 'If I would've known how hard it would be to take care of a blind woman, I woulda asked Jesus to bring me a better wife!'"

"Oh, no, he didn't!" I felt my face boiling and yet Momma May smiled.

"When people are angry, they say things they don't always mean . . . especially men. Oh, I gave him the silent treatment for a whole week. I told him if he thought it was hard being married to a blind woman, let's see how it was to be married to one who's blind and mute."

I laughed. "I bet he ain't like that."

"Not one bit. But it made him appreciate me more, knowing that things could always be worse. He apologized, said he'd been overloaded with stress at work and took it out on me. He said it was nothing but the devil trying to take away the only good thing in life. Plus, I took a deeper look into my situation and realized I wasn't being the woman I needed to be. So I got myself up and learned my way around that house. It improved our marriage."

I dropped my head. "And, let me guess, you think I should forgive Dante."

"Yes. He doesn't understand why you don't like to go to church like I do, Hope. Let him see from your eyes."

"So, does that mean you understand my point of view in that situation?" I asked.

"I understand both points of view, Hope. Dante's birthday present to you wasn't inside of that church, it was helping you get over your greatest fear. I actually gave him the idea, however, he didn't implement it correctly. Hope, you will have to face your fears head-on. You can pray for deliverance all day long but God is not going to force you into it. Sometimes He will. But in this case, you have to walk into it. You have to be stronger than your fears or you'll never be the woman of God He intends for you to be. Do you understand that, Hope?"

"Yes, ma'am."

"And don't worry, sweetie. I got on Dante about that mouth and anger of his. He knows he was wrong."

"Well, I still ain't ready to forgive him."

"In due time, you will."

Momma May and I spent the rest of the day talking about anything and everything until it tired her out, which didn't take long. She was such a wise woman, almost as if God Himself spoke every word from her mouth. She had a story for everything, and every story was meant to teach. Every story had a way of wrapping itself around my heart, feeding it with truth. And that's what God teaches us. We are to use our words to lift people up, not tear them down. That was the difference between my birth mother and my spiritual mother. My birth mother only spoke words meant to tear me down. Everything she said was from the devil. She wanted to keep me low so that I wouldn't ever be able to walk into my greatness. The devil has a powerful influence over those who give him that power. But now I stepped on the devil's head daily. He would not be victorious.

Surprisingly, Dante was sitting on the porch as I walked up to the house later that night. I could tell by his low head, the way his shoulders slouched, that he felt remorse. *Good.*

It was a beautiful night. John had once said, "The sound of nature is at its best once the sun goes down. Every day life tends to distract us from the beauty of life, the things that bring true joy. We tend to miss out on the secrets of nature, things long forgotten from ancient times. Like how soothing it is to listen to grasshopper's music, to the owls hooting in nearby trees, to the critters rummaging about in bushes. And the stars seemed to shine brighter at night."

"Hey," Dante said, eying me warily.

I fought down the urge to be difficult and settled for a "Hi."

"Are you just now getting back from the hospital?"

"Yeah, because somebody was acting funny." *Welp, there goes my attempt at not being difficult.*

Dante sighed. "I'm sorry . . . for everything I said. I didn't mean any of it."

"Whatever, Dante. I don't even care anymore. It is what it is."

I took a seat next to him and stared out at the dark night. I remember being a kid and looking up to the sky, wondering what all was out there. *The stars are much brighter in the country; the city lights are too distracting. People decorate the city in lights and forget about the stars and moon. We'd rather busy ourselves with Times Square than sitting under the sky, learning the constellations.*

Society has a way of distracting us from the things that really mean the most. Children are too consumed by video games and television to go outside and play. Adults would rather watch someone else's reality on TV than create their own. What happened to spending all day outside? I remember the joy of it. Now we complain about cramped legs from sitting on the couch all day. We're fatter than we used to be. We're never satisfied because we're brainwashed to think something better is around the corner. A new phone, a new car, a new sandwich at some fast food restaurant. Has technology replaced God? Has money? Have we replaced ourselves with something less human?

I made a promise to myself to stay true to nature. So when I looked at the stars and was reminded of how humans had regressed over the centuries, I clung to them. *They are constant. When everything around me changes, the stars, they stay the same. Kinda like God.*

But all stars die and He lives forever.

Maybe it's actually a big difference.

"What are you looking at?" Dante asked, following my eyes up to the sky.

"The stars. Do you ever wonder what's all out there?"

"Everything," he responded. "Hopes, dreams, the future, our prayers."

I nodded. "Do you think God lives in outer space?"

"I think He lives beyond it. There's so much we just can't see, or possibly begin to understand. But I think God is beyond the stars and galaxies."

"Why do you think He created all of the stars and other planets if He was just going to use the earth?"

"That's a question you have to save for God. He has a lot of things He plans on sharing with us."

I guessed that was as good an answer as any. Maybe God would share all of His secrets with us like an episode of *How It's Made.*

Science has gone a long way, but we can't possibly begin to understand all of the universe's ways. Some scientists are so convinced in their science that they ignore the fact that there is a God. Science is just a way for our human minds to understand how God created everything. Regardless, people never want to give God credit for His works. That was something Momma May taught me during those long visiting hours at the church. She was so full of wisdom.

I hadn't realized how much I'd learned just by being in her presence. I'd find myself referencing her teachings throughout my day. Well, God worked her teachings into my heart and I'd take them wherever I went.

I instantly felt said, just thinking about Momma May.

The doctors sad her condition was worsening each day. They had managed to get the blood flow back on track to where she didn't need any machines, but her body was beginning to shut down. Her skin started to look gray and she began losing her hair. I noticed once while brushing it.

But even though Momma May was dying, her spirit was still fresh. She still taught me the importance of life: to love God, to love all of His children as I loved myself, and to bring others to Christ. The last part I hadn't really figured out. I couldn't even step foot inside of a church to bring others to Christ. I thought only preachers did that. I guessed I still had a lot to learn.

"What are you thinking about?" Dante asked. I'd almost forgotten he was sitting beside me.

I sighed. "Life."

Chapter 20

Dante came jogging up to the house that morning, the way he always did. I had been sitting on the porch, thinking about my future, when his voice sounded.

"Good morning!" he sang.

I frowned. "Why you so happy for?" I asked.

"I got a surprise for us after we go visit Momma May today."

"Well, tell me now. I hate surprises."

He shook his head. "Nope. You have to wait and find out," he stated irrevocability.

I sighed and stood. "Fine . . . and it better be good."

An hour later we walked through the hospital doors. The moment I entered, I felt something off. Something . . . unsettling. I couldn't put my finger on it. I looked over at Dante, who seemed oblivious to what I felt. Dread, was it? Sometimes our soul foresees pain that our brains have yet to recognize.

When we got on the elevator, I stood back, fiddling with my fingers. Dante noticed and frowned, but he said nothing. When the elevator doors opened, I rushed out, nearly knocking Dante over.

"Dang," he said, righting himself.

"I'm sorry," I breathed, barely above a whisper. "I just . . . I feel . . . Can I go see Momma May first today?"

He frowned. "Yeah, but what's wrong?"

I shrugged. "I don't know," I said and took off toward the swinging doors that led me to Momma May. I turned down a few hallways and almost bumped into a few people who had come from Momma May's room. I guessed they were church members.

I stood in front of it, wondering if I should knock. The thought lasted only a few seconds before I went ahead and allowed myself in her room.

And she lay there, half asleep. She looked up at me with a smile. My raging heart settled as I came to her bed. I ran a hand over her gray, thinning hair.

"Every morning I wake up and thank God that you are in my life," I told her. I took a seat next to her, studying her pale face. She looked thinner today, more sickly. There was a bedpan sitting on the other side of her, which let me know she'd been getting sick. Momma May smiled and opened her mouth to say something but couldn't.

She'd never been this bad.

I stood up and walked to the door, yelling out, "Nurse!"

A pretty lady with a bright smile came up to me just seconds later. "How can I help you?" she asked.

"Yeah, she's not talking. She was talking fine yesterday. Why can't she talk today?"

The nurse reached behind me and grabbed Momma May's chart. "Stage four cancer," she said, skimming over the papers. "This is quite normal once a patient's health declines. She'll have trouble remembering things, difficulty concentrating, problems with speech. She's weak. Do you understand that?"

I shook my head. "A person's condition doesn't worsen overnight."

She smiled apologetically. "Tell that to God."

I frowned as the nurse walked away. Tell that to God? What did that even mean? Tell that to the person who was in charge so they could fix it? It wasn't like God would just change Momma May's condition. I'd prayed and prayed for Momma May to get better until I realized I was praying the wrong thing. And then I prayed to allow His will to be done, whether it meant healing Momma May or not. And then I started praying for her to go peacefully with the least amount of pain possible.

I sat back down next to Momma May and held her hand. I tried not to let the tears come out.

"I felt something funny when I came to the hospital. I thought something was wrong with you. And now you ain't talking." I paused, trying to compose myself before I cried all over Momma May. The last thing she'd want was me crying because of her. She wanted me strong and I'd be that, even if I had to fake it. "I wish you could tell me another story, but I'm being selfish. How about I tell you a story, Momma May?

"I told you a story already but you was asleep. It was easier that way, because I didn't want you to judge me. But I know now that you won't. You ain't like my momma. You're better than her. You gave me a place to stay. You taught me about a God who really does love me. You showed me how to be a better person and to let go of my past. I'm so thankful."

I went on to explain the things that hurt most. About how verbally abusive Momma was; however, I went into more detail with her that I'd ever done with anyone. I finished my story with, "That's it. That's about as deep as my story gets. I was scared that you would judge me."

Momma May opened her mouth to speak but struggled. I could tell by how much she strained that she needed to tell me something. "I . . . al . . . ready . . . kn . . . knew."

I frowned. "How?"

"I . . . was . . . wasn't . . . 'sl . . . 'sleep."

I almost cried. This whole time I had been keeping that one secret from Momma May, afraid she'd kick me out or judge me. She knew and it didn't change a thing. She still loved me, unconditionally. The pain of knowing she'd soon be gone engulfed me. I choked on a sob.

I grabbed on to Momma May's hand, watching the machine that monitored her heart rate. I hadn't noticed how much it had slowed down in the last few minutes. I didn't know if it was normal. *Maybe I should alert the nurses.* But I locked eyes with Momma May as she tried to lift her hand from mine to wipe my tears away. How did she know I was crying?

"D . . . don't."

"No. I should be telling you that! Don't." I paused. I was on the verge of a breakdown. I didn't want her to hear my voice wavering. I needed her to believe I was strong enough. I inhaled, stabilizing myself. "Don't die. Please stay. I still need you."

She tried to shake her head. "Strong," she muttered.

"I'm not strong. Not without you."

"G . . ." She started coughing. Once it settled, she tried to speak again. "God."

I didn't understand what she meant, but I nodded anyway. I could tell how much it hurt her not to be able to speak to me the way she wanted to. Momma May used to be a lively older woman. One who would walk into a room and command attention with her presence alone. One would know, just by being in the same room with her, that God stood near her. His spirit was all over her. And it still was, but it no longer kept her strong. Instead, it allowed her to weaken. God was calling Momma May home. I could feel it. I knew the moment I walked into the hospital that something was off. Yeah, God was in this place, claiming His prize, claiming Momma May. I should have been okay with that, knowing Momma May was going to heaven, but I couldn't let her go. I wasn't okay. She was mine! She needed to fight for her life!

I remembered a poem by Dylan Thomas that I read in high school. The teacher told us to write a one-page essay about the meaning behind the poem "Do Not Go

Gentle into That Good Night." I remember writing "I don't know" until I filled up the whole paper. I never really cared for poems and their misguided meanings. I was never smart enough to figure them out. But, I realized, some poems were so deep we couldn't begin to understand the meaning without actually experiencing it for ourselves. Well, now I understood the poem clearly as Momma May lay there, dying. She probably didn't have a week left, let alone a few days. And yet, she seemed gentle, almost willing to go.

The poem was about a man sitting at his father's deathbed, trying to convince him why he shouldn't die quietly. Fight! Rage! Do anything, but don't go gentle into that good night. Even the old, the good, the grave, and the wild men fought. No matter what lives they lived, they fought against death. Nobody wants to die. So I understood what the author meant.

He wanted his father to fight because he didn't want to lose him to the dying of light, which was death. And I didn't want to lose Momma May. But I'd understand why she'd go peacefully. She knew she was going to heaven. For her, it was a joyous thing and she would go gently.

I felt her slipping away.

"Don't go gentle, Momma May," I cried. "I love you, okay? Just hang in for a while longer."

Her hands squeezed around mine. "Love . . . you."

Moments later the heart monitor began beeping as Momma May closed her eyes. I didn't have time to process what was going on as the nurses and doctors rushed in the room, trying to pry me from Momma May. I would've fought them, but they were the only ones who could help her. Before I knew it, I was pushed into the hallway with the door slammed in my face. I stood in shock for a few moments before I turned around to face Dante.

"I saw the nurses rushing in," he said, wide-eyed and worried. "What's going on?"

"Her . . . her . . ."

"Come on, Hope!"

I sighed. "The heart monitor started beeping. I don't know what's wrong. They all rushed in and kicked me out," I told him.

He nodded once and pulled me away from the room, passed the nurse's desk and out of the swinging doors into the lobby. He stopped and spun around to face me, cupping my face in his hands. His serious eyes held mine as he studied me.

"Don't break down, Hope," he whispered. "No matter what happens, promise me you'll be strong. Even for me." He choked on his words. "Hope, I know how you feel. She's all I have too. I don't have family to lean on. I only had my mom and she's gone. If Pastor May dies, I only have you. And we have to be strong together."

I nodded, but I knew it wasn't a promise I could keep. If Momma May died, so would the good in my life. *I might as well go back home to that sad, poor house with a crazy momma and beg for her to take me back.* I'd have put up with all of her craziness if it meant not being alone.

But deep down, I knew I wasn't alone.

I had Dante.

Momma May said we'd one day get married. The thought once brought me joy, but nothing could wipe out the sense of dread that began at the bottom of my heart. It was filling up, almost pouring over. I couldn't take it!

"Don't, Hope," he said, turning my face back to meet his eyes. "I see you wavering, giving up, and losing hope. But you can't lose hope, do you know why?" I shook my head. "Because you *are* hope. You give me hope. You've given Pastor May hope."

"How?"

Dante smiled. "Pastor May told me she prayed to God daily to be able to help someone like you. Help them find God. She said it's one of the most important things to do on earth. We have to bring as many people back to God as possible. And she had an ache to change someone's life. She knew she was old, didn't have much time. She wanted to give someone every good thing God had given to her. Which was the spirit of grace, knowledge, and wisdom, so that you may pass it on to others and so that they will pass it on to more. It is the gift that keeps on giving. So Pastor May prayed for a girl to pass everything on to, and she handed the torch to you. Do you know what that means, now?"

I shook my head.

"It means it will soon be your turn to spread the gospel, to tell others about your testimony, to show little girls who know no love God's love. That's the point. God loves all of us, even when we are a mess. Even when we sin. Even when we don't even acknowledge Him in all of our ways. And He's there for people when they decide to turn to Him. But He needs people like you to tell others about Him, so that they may have eternal life. There will be a little girl much like yourself who needs to know that she can make it too. You're meant to give the world hope in a God who loves all."

And all this time, I wondered why I couldn't be Faith, the good twin. All this time I thought she had the better name. I thought Faith trumped Hope, and maybe in ways it did, but the word "hope" was used in the Bible as well. Jeremiah 29:11:

> *For I know the plans I have for you, declares the Lord, plans for welfare and not for evil, to give you a future and a hope.*

Maybe God was speaking directly to me when He said that. So I nodded, pushing all of my dread back into a place where I kept it safely locked away. "I understand," I told Dante.

"Good," he said, letting go of me. His face turned sad. "Because I have a feeling she's not going to make it."

Chapter 21

The doctors were able to stabilize Momma May, which made me think everything was going to be okay. But we got a knock on the door late that night. Dante had fallen asleep on the couch downstairs and I had just finished throwing on my pajamas. I heard Dante get up and answer the door. I left my room and jogged down the steps. I paused when I saw Norma standing outside. Norma didn't usually knock since it was her momma's house and she had a key. I hadn't seen her since the last incident with Momma May's safe.

Her eyes were red and her cheeks were puffy from crying. She looked up at me with apologetic eyes and cleared her throat. "Can I come in?" Dante stood aside and let her walk in. She passed us and took a seat in the living room. We followed suit and sat down.

"So." Norma avoided looking either of us in our eyes. She fiddled with her fingers and shook in places I'd never seen someone shake. Either she was coming off of a high or she was in pain. I hoped it was the high. "I got a call from the doctor about an hour ago. They told me Momma had another stroke. They said her body completely shut off." She choked on her words. "The cancer had run its course. Momma passed away at nine-oh-two tonight. There was nothing they could do."

My world tore at its core and every good thing leaked out, like liquid from a broken glass. I couldn't salvage it even if I wanted to. Everything. Gone. Right when I believed God granted us more time.

God.

I felt furious toward Him. I wanted to yell at Him for taking her away from me. I only had her for nine months. He would have her for an eternity. *Why, God? Huh? Why would you do this to me? Why would you give me joy only to take it away? What about me and my feelings? How do you expect me to get through this? I hate this world and everything in it. Just take me too! Take me too!*

But I didn't dare say that out loud, not after I promised Dante I'd be strong. And he sat beside me, squeezing my leg, holding on to me because he had nothing left to hold on to. Not even his own sanity. He started to cry first, wrapping his arms around me, rocking back and forth, praying and cursing all the same. And I sat there with dry eyes and a blank stare. I wouldn't cry, for fear of never-ending tears. My eyes would run like deep waters and it wouldn't stop until the whole world was drowning in my sorrow. I decided to direct my emotions at someone else. Norma.

"You're crying like you care. The only thing you care about is that coke!" I said.

"Hope!" Dante warned.

"No, it's okay," Norma said to him. "I understand. You're mad, angry at the world because a woman who you only knew for a few months has died."

"It was nine months," I corrected.

"I knew her for forty years!"

"And half those years you dedicated to stealing from her!" I yelled back.

"Stop!" Dante shouted, standing between us. "Do you think this is what Pastor May would've wanted? We all have our flaws, Hope. Don't judge her. Pastor May didn't."

I laughed. "Oh, look at Dante coming to the rescue. Pure-hearted, perfect, Ivy League Dante."

"Do you think I want her here? No! I don't! But it's not about me, or you. Pastor May just died. Hope, just go to your room or something. I'll handle this."

"But—"

"Go!" he said with so much authority, I thought I was staring at a different person. But he was right. I was just trying to take the pain I felt and redirect it to Norma.

"I'm sorry," I told her. "I'll pray that God takes care of you and heals your addiction." I went up to my room and collapsed on my bed and tried to cry for Momma May. But I couldn't.

I was too numb.

The next few days blew by like a dream. I watched as people came to Momma May's house, offering food and condolences. People who I'd never met. But they knew me by name and they hugged and prayed over me like I was one of their own. It made me feel good knowing Momma May surrounded herself with people who loved just as she did.

I ran into Joyce again. She was the woman I'd met at the hospital, Momma May's friend from her church. She was beautiful and dark, with long, graying hair and a warm smile. She took me out back, away from everyone who crowded the house, and sat me down in a lawn chair.

It was a beautiful day, which was ironic, due to the fact that Momma May had just died. It's funny how the world carries on unfazed by our pain. The sun shined brightly above us as if Momma May hadn't passed away. The birds chirped away in nearby trees, creating music I once cherished. I spotted a couple of daisies in the yard that seemed to bloom overnight. But none of it mattered without Momma May. I wished I could've given her my eyesight just so she'd see the beauty of the world one last time before she died.

Joyce sat adjacent to me and reached into her purse, pulling out an envelope. "Here," she said, handing me the envelope. "May asked me to hold on to this and give it to you after she passed away. I used to come up to the hospital and write letters for her, helped her redo her will, get all of her debts straightened out. Momma May left behind a fortune. Did you know that? Well, I don't think her kids even knew.

"When her husband died, May didn't know how she was going to pay off her bills and afford to bury him. But many people paid their respects, literally. She got all kinds of donations to the church and to her specifically. She got letters in the mail and when she opened them, hundred dollar bills would drop out. One day she came home and found a check written out to her for ten thousand dollars. Ain't God good?"

"The money she got for the church, she used for the church, and the money she got for personal reasons, she used to pay off the debt and save. She told me she kept a safe in her room with all of that money. She said some of it started to go missing whenever Norma came over."

"It's because she stole some of it. She's a cokehead."

"And May knew that. That's why she put the money in a safer place. She left me in charge of her will," she said, handing me the letter.

I turned it over, smiling at Momma May's handwriting. It said, "Hope." I should have been happy but my head wouldn't stop pounding. Momma May was gone, and in my hand I held all that she'd left me. I didn't want it. I wanted her, not some stupid note giving me some money or something.

"Thanks, but—"

"No," she said, cutting me off. "May said you'd try to reject it."

"I don't want it."

"Read the letter. I'm sure it will change your mind." Joyce smiled sympathetically and stood. "Please read everything, Hope. It's what May would've wanted. Do this for her."

I nodded and watched her walk away. I fiddled with the note in my hand, wondering if I should open it now or wait. If I opened it, I'd probably spend the rest of the day outside, crying and rereading it over. The people inside would start to wonder about me. They'd come looking for me and find me out here being dramatic. I'd keep this for a more private, intimate moment.

Later that night, after everyone finally went home and all who were left were Dante and me, I snuck off to my room. I shut my door quietly behind me and sat down on my bed. I had placed the note under my pillow earlier, and now retrieved it. I stared again at the handwriting. It was amazing how something so insignificant like someone's handwriting could stir up so much emotion inside of me. But every little thing that reminded me of Momma May did.

Dante said I was taking it well, whatever that meant. Who takes death well? So because I wasn't screaming and causing a scene I was handling it well? Little did he know the pain I was feeling. The emptiness. The saying "two steps forward, three steps back" fit my situation perfectly. I moved ahead two steps when I found Momma May that day while she was going to her car. And when she offered me a place to live. But just I fell back three steps.

Where was I going to live? What was I going to do without her? I had only a few hundred dollars left from the money Momma May had given me. That would buy me a week in a motel, but after that? Yes, Dante had a house, but I don't think God would approve of me staying with a man. And then there was always home, back in the country, with Momma and Faith.

I missed Faith. I missed our long conversations. I missed her telling me about the Bible. I hadn't even realized how much I learned about God through her. I missed our walks to the church on Sunday mornings when I'd drop her off and go sit under my peach tree. Everything about my sister, I missed. But it wasn't enough to make me go home to Momma. She wouldn't let me if I tried.

I sighed and began opening the letter. I would have rather not thought about the future at the moment. I'd busy myself with whatever Momma May felt she needed to tell me. A note fell onto my lap, along with a key. I frowned, picking up the key, wondering where it went to. I set it beside me and unfolded the note and began reading:

My dearest Hope,
Once I lost my husband, my world darkened. Believe me when I tell you, I started living the motions. For years I got up in the mornings, ate, played checkers, watched my soaps, and napped. The rest of my day past by until it was bedtime. I didn't feel. I practically watched my own grandbaby steal from me and I did nothing. I almost wanted my life to end. I even lost touch with my church members. But I prayed for God to bring meaning again into my life. Well, He answered. The day you came into my life was the day I felt energized again, like God was building me up for another mission, my last one. He called to me, telling me to take you in, give you a place to stay, and to teach you and just love you. I said, "God, I will do anything you ask me to." And so I opened my heart to you, and by doing that, I opened myself up to God.

But you were a challenge, Hope. Half of the time, I didn't know if I wanted to hug you or hit you. Once I realized how damaged you were I said, "God, how do you expect me to change her?" And He said, "Speak wisdom, knowledge, and love on to her and I will allow it to manifest." My God!

And so I did what He told me to. I started to tell you stories about my life, things you'd relate to. I opened you up to grow, afraid because I thought that once I was done doing what God asked me to He'd take you away from me. Little did I know, it would be me who was taken from you. I was more upset that I'd be leaving you than I was about passing away. I prayed to God to give me just one more day. Let me love Hope one more day. And He did. I'm sitting here in this hospital bed, praising God for another day with you, baby. I love you like a daughter and I hope that you feel that love, even after I've passed. Continue to live life with love and give to others the gift that God allowed me to give to you.

You're probably wondering what the key is for. It belongs to the safe in my room. Please open it. I am trusting you to make sure my last wishes are met. I hope you find joy in what I've left you. And Hope, please go to church. God has a purpose for you in His holy temple.

With love, the deepest kind,
Momma May

I read the note at least five more times before I was satisfied. It almost made me feel like each time that I read it she was sitting next to me, saying it out loud. I would read this letter every night if it meant that I'd have her close again.

I eventually got up and went into her room. I walked over to the picture that hid the safe and removed it. I hadn't noticed that little keyhole at the bottom of the safe when Norma had been trying to open it. I placed the key inside of the lock and turned. The safe clicked open. Another letter sat neatly folded inside. I retrieved the note and took a seat on Momma May's bed. I tried to block her smell, which would've caused tears. I didn't want to cry. I opened the note, wanting to read it, but I couldn't bring myself to it.

"What are you doing?" Dante asked from the door. He looked from me to the open safe and then back to me with suspicion.

I held up the key. "Joyce, she gave me a note Momma May left me and this key was in here." I held up the new letter. "This is her will."

Dante rushed into the room and took a seat next to me. "Did you read it?"

I shook my head. I couldn't bring myself to read it. "Can you?" I asked, handing it over to him.

Dante grabbed the letter, skimming over it. "Um, she left some money to her kids and grandkids. It says, 'To Dante, I leave my house and all the things in it. May you build a beautiful family and raise them there, as I've raised mine. It is a blessed house. And to Hope, I leave my church. I have changed the name to Rising Hope Ministries. You may not understand why I've given you the church, but one day you will.'"

I almost fainted. "She left me the church? Why would she do that? Why would I want her church?" I asked angrily.

Dante's face reddened. "That's so selfish. She just died and left you her church and you're mad? I told her you weren't going to understand but she was so bent on it. Just like how she thought you'd go to church on your birthday. You want to know why I was so mad that day? Momma May asked me to do it because she didn't want her death to be the reason why you finally stepped foot into a church. But what scared her most was wondering if you'd bail on her funeral because of your fear. You're so selfish."

I felt horrible. Of course, it all made sense now. Dante had been so angry that day because he was only trying to honor Momma May's wish, and he couldn't. But I didn't know. She didn't tell me.

"She should've told me, Dante! How was I supposed to know that?" I cried. I was so frustrated at messing everything up. "I'm sorry. If I would've known, I would've gone. I'm so stupid."

"Hey," Dante sighed, pulling me close. "Stop crying, it's okay. Just accept her gift. She has a reason for it and I'll explain all of it when we go to her funeral. She wouldn't want you to beat yourself up."

"I know." I sniffed. "I just could've done things differently."

"It's never too late when you're still breathing," he assured me.

And he was right.

The day of the funeral came quickly, and with it came dread. I woke up groggy and tired from tossing and turning all night. I went into my closet, pulled out a black dress I had bought the day before, and laid it on my bed. After I showered and dressed, I joined Dante downstairs in the kitchen. He handed me a cup of hot coffee.

"I figured you didn't sleep good."

"Thanks," I said, taking the cup, but I was too anxious to even drink. Today was her funeral. At her church. The church I'd never stepped foot in due to fear. It was the reason I'd tossed and turned all night. If I slept, I'd wake up to the worst day of my life, so I tried not to sleep.

Dante could sense my hesitation and sighed. "You don't have to go."

"I want to," I told him. Even though I was afraid, I needed to say good-bye to her.

An hour later we stood in front of the entrance of the church. It looked the same as I remembered it, but the clouds hung low above, adding strange shadows over the building. It had started raining on the ride to the church and I wondered if it was God Himself mourning.

I watched as people piled inside the church and was amazed by how many people showed up. There had to be at least a hundred people. And I watched them all looking sad with lowered heads and humbled hearts as I wondered each of their significance in Momma May's life. Most of them probably went to her church, but some of them would be family and I knew they felt ten times worse than I did. I wished I could console them.

"Come on," Dante said, tugging my arm, and I sucked in a huge breath and stepped onto the church grounds. That was the first step. I tried to keep my breathing even and my hands from nervously fiddling as a very sad memory flooded my thoughts.

I was seven years old again. Sitting on the couch, watching Faith wait for Grandma on Easter Sunday. She was excited about an Easter egg hunt that the church was having for the kids. Momma had made her an Easter basket with all types of candy and suckers, small toys and crayons. I eyed her with envy as she grabbed another piece of candy, popping it into her mouth. Same thing happened last year. I hoped this year would be different.

"Faith, stop eating that candy." Momma came out of the kitchen, grabbing the piece of candy out of Faith's hand. "You're gonna get that pretty white dress dirty."

"Can I eat some candy, Momma? I ain't got a dress on to get dirty," I asked with anticipation.

I hadn't learned yet to never expect anything from that woman.

"No," she yelled. *"How many times do I gotta tell you? You can't have no candy. Faith gets an Easter basket because she's going to church."*

"Well, can I go to church then?"

Momma looked at me with the most evil glint in her eyes. She took in a deep breath, trying to keep herself from exploding. She came up to me with her face inches from my hopeful, innocent face. "If you step foot in a church, you'll burn."

I jerked out of the memory as Dante and I were about to enter the church. I stopped and stepped aside, allowing a few other people to go before me. I didn't realize I was shaking until Dante grabbed both of my hands, steadying them.

"Just breath, Hope."

"The devil can't go to church," I said, recalling the recent memory.

"What?"

"That's what Momma said," I cried. I was sure the people walking up to the church would think I was crying for Momma May, and in ways I was. How did I think I was strong enough to go to church today? I couldn't do it. "She put it in my head, the fear. It's all because of her! I can't do it."

"Your mom wanted you to be just like her, which is nothing. But you're everything, Hope. I love you."

My eyes shot up, meeting his with curiosity.

"I do. Ever since the first day I met you. I could see God's grace all over you. I could see why Pastor May took to you. The problem is, your mom brainwashed you into believing you're not good enough for God. But you are. You're everything to Him. He died for you. The devil works on us harder when he knows God has great plans for us. He started with you at a young age, tried to keep you from church, because it's the place where God meant for you to thrive. Do you want to know why Pastor May gave you this church? It's because your calling is to be a pastor, just like her. Do you think your life was a coincidence? No. Don't you see? It's all part of His perfect plan. This . . ." He pointed to the church. "This is your destiny. You were called into ministry, and, Hope, your testimony is great."

I fell to my knees, overtaken by God's love. It had always been with me. It urged me forward when I thought I'd never make it. It caressed me on those nights when I couldn't stand to be alone. His love sheltered me when I was homeless with nowhere to go. It protected me from Momma's beatings and cruelty day by day. It comforted me on those Sunday mornings when I sat under the peach tree, thinking He never loved me. Oh God! How wonderful, how beautiful is His love, grace, and mercy! He was here this whole time and never let me go. I didn't deserve His blessings and mercy and yet He still accepted me as his child in Jesus' name. He found favor in me when no one else did. He accepted me when everyone else rejected me. I owed my life to Him.

And in that moment, I made a decision.

I stood up, dusted myself off, and I walked into that church. My church.

My destiny.

Epilogue

Ten years passed by beautifully and the good Lord never stopped blessing our lives. Dante and I got married when I turned nineteen; we had our first child when I was twenty-one. We named her May because she was a blessing, just like Momma May. It was a name we agreed on the first day I found out I was having a girl. And May was a joy. Her laughter brought a new meaning of happiness into our lives. I loved spoiling her and giving her the things my mother never gave to me. I taught her, the way Momma May taught me. I gave her everything I wasn't able to my first unborn.

I managed to get back in school after Momma May passed away. When I graduated I went to college for ministry. Dante had finished school way before I did, and led the church. I was his first lady. I spent a lot of time working with the youth, helping them build relationships with God. World change begins in our youth; they are the ones who grow to lead our countries. If we catch them early and teach them Jesus' ways, we could prevent so much crime in the future.

And that's what I tried to do. I'd reach out to foster homes, shelters, schools, anywhere to get to the children. We started a great youth program that I led every Sunday. Children of all ages and from all walks of life would come to hear me preach and they would always leave with hearts opened to God.

I gave all of the glory to Him.

Norma was delivered right before my eyes one Sunday morning. She burst through the church doors, crying and screaming for God to deliver her. Dante laid his hands on her and the Holy Spirit took over. She'd now been clean for five years and had been a great member to our church.

I wish I could say that my sister and I reunited the right way, but we didn't. I tried calling the house but the number was changed. I drove by a few times, but no one was ever home. I wrote her letters with a return address, and she never wrote me back. My biggest regret was ruining my relationship with my own twin, but I had to have faith that if God wanted us to be reunited, then we would. One day, years after Momma May passed, I got a letter in the mail addressed to me. It was from my sister.

I hurriedly opened it, trying to hold back my tears of joy. It had been ten years since I saw my twin's face. *Separated by catastrophe, but we'll soon be brought together by love.* I'd dreamt of this day for years. I'd hoped she heard stories of my success and would come find me, but that never happened.

I pulled the letter out of the envelope and opened it.

> *Hope, my sister,*
> *Please meet me by that old peach tree near the church next Sunday at 8:00 a.m.*
> *Faith*

I ran inside of the house, passed my daughter, who was watching TV, and ran into the kitchen, where my husband was cooking May's lunch. He turned around, smiling like he always did when he saw me. I smiled back, holding up the letter.

"Faith."

He dropped the grilled cheese sandwich back on the pan in shock. "After all these years?"

I nodded. "Finally."
Dante pulled me into a hug, as if he'd never let go.

That Sunday, I stood alone, staring at the peach tree, which held so many distant, yet strong memories. I closed my eyes, listening to the sound of nature, which hadn't changed since I last remembered. The feeling of anticipation was building up in my stomach. I couldn't wait to see her, to touch her, to cry with her. I wanted to tell my sister that everything turned out fine for me, that the day I walked out of Momma's house, I walked into a blessing.

I felt a presence behind me, or maybe I felt the wind blowing past. However, I turned around and saw Momma. She was much older than I remembered, with wrinkles swallowing her fragile face. It had only been ten years and yet her back was hunched over from working so hard. Instinct told me to run to her, take her in my arms, and hold her. It'd been years since I saw her face. However, I couldn't bring myself to hug a woman who never seemed to love me.

I smeared tears into my skin as I tried to wipe them away. *Faith.* I needed my sister. "Momma, where's Faith?"

Momma shook her head. I knew what she'd say even before the words slurred out of her mouth: "Faith is gone. She went to be with the Lord."

The pain of an incident becomes faded with time, distancing itself like an aloof and shy child. It's the memory that lingers, a venomous snake waiting for an opportunity to strike. I was sure that if my soul were visible, it'd have been masked with battle wounds. But I wore those scars proudly. They were reminders that I'd made it, that I was still making it. The devil was not successful in his pursuit to destroy me.

"How?"

"Giving birth. Two twin girls. She named them before she passed. She named them Hope and Faith."

I groaned in pain, almost collapsing to the ground. *My sister! She's dead.* I almost knew she'd live this long, wonderful life and have plenty of kids and that we'd reunite and move next door to each other and raise our families together. But no, she was now gone. And after ten years, she hadn't even tried to look for me.

"I wrote the letter, Hope. I needed to see you. I wanted to—"

"You," I said, cutting her off. My sorrow turned to anger in a matter of seconds. "It's your fault! You took my sister away from me and now it's too late!"

"I'm sorry," she alleged, letting tears fall from her eyes. I could almost see the regret seeping out of her skin. It lightened my heart, but not enough. "I'm sorry for everything I did to you."

"Why did you do it?" I asked. I needed to know that it was never me. That the reason she never loved me wasn't because I was bad or evil.

Momma lowered her head and slumped her shoulders in guilt. She then looked up to the peach tree, as if the answer lay there. I too looked at the tree, wondering how old it was, how many stories it held. This tree and its fruit had been a home and a way of life for many animals. The peaches didn't grow as ripe as they once had when I was younger. Maybe it was because I caused the tree to die a little.

I'd planted the seed of hatred toward my momma right here. This was where I cried out all of my hurt, and this was where I had to go back to in order to completely move forward from my past. I watched Momma as she began to explain why she never seemed to love me.

"My mom hated me. She used to say all sorts of messed-up stuff to me when I was younger. She called me a devil, too. She'd beat me for it. She got pregnant with me and her momma didn't like the boy, said he was a devil and his seed would be too. My daddy left my momma and me, and she began to believe I was an abomination. I did the same to you. I thought you were the result of my sins.

"I thought I was only having one baby and then you came. I should've been happy but every time I looked in your eyes, I saw a spitting image of myself. I saw a bad omen. I believed there was a generational curse, one passed down from mother to daughter, and I just knew I passed it to you. In my mind, I was no longer the devil, it was your turn. You looked just like me. It was so easy to pass it on to you." Her head dropped even lower. "I'm the devil."

"Momma—"

"I *am* the devil!" she screamed. "The things I did to you and you were so innocent. I hate myself for it. I won't ever forgive myself."

My anger vanished and I knew God was taking over. I could feel Him all around us, encouraging me to do the right thing. I reached out to mother and wrapped her in my arms and held her tight. I couldn't believe I was doing it, hugging her, loving her when she didn't deserve it, but it was the kind of thing the Lord would do and I tried to obey Him in all of my ways.

"I always kept enough love in my heart for a day like this. I forgive you, Momma," I cried. "God forgives you. You have to forgive yourself."

She pulled back, staring at me like a small child. "Do you think He will?"

Just then, I heard the choir begin to sing. I listened closely as the song filled my heart with recognition. I knew it all too well, sang it so many times I could recite it in my sleep.

"Do you hear it?" I asked her, watching her eyes look around until they landed on the church in the distance. It was an old spiritual song about being saved.

I took Momma's hands into my own and lifted them in the air. I knew what Jesus wanted me to do.

"Momma, have you ever been saved? Have you been to church since I left?"

She shook her head sadly. "But I want to know Jesus."

"Then repeat after me." I recited the salvation prayer, listening as Momma sang it back to me, shaking. Halfway through, the Holy Spirit took over and Momma started shouting and speaking in tongues, praising God. And I joined her, thanking Him, even though I lost Momma May and my sister. I thanked Him for reuniting my mother and me. I thanked Him for my wonderful husband and beautiful daughter and my sister's twins, who I couldn't wait to meet. I thanked Him for the children's lives I'd been able to touch over the years. I also thanked Him for the years to come, and I hoped it would be a lot more.

Momma and I stayed under the peach tree for a long time, praising a God who had always been there. Praising a God who never let us go.

Reader Group
Guide Questions

1. Why is the book titled *Under the Peach Tree?* Use references in the book to support your answer.
2. What is the significance of the peach tree? Why did it have so much meaning?
3. Who was to blame for the intimate relationship between Hope and John? Why?
4. Do you think Faith cared more about her dresses and gifts, or more about her sister, Hope? Explain why.
5. Hope felt as though God was never a part of her life in the beginning. In what ways did He show Himself to her throughout her childhood?
6. Should John have run off with Hope when she told him that she was pregnant or stay with Momma? Why?
7. How did Momma May help Hope grow as a person? Use references in the book to support your answer.
8. Dante and Hope seemed to have a love/hate friendship throughout the book. At what point did it grow in to a deep love?
9. What purpose did the following characters, Momma, Faith, John, Momma May, and Dante, serve in Hope's life?
10. What is the moral/message of the story?

About the Author

Charlay Marie always knew she wanted to be an author, having gained Internet raves over her fan fiction stories as a teenager. Seeing how well she could move her readers, she continued writing her first Christian fiction novel, *Under the Peach Tree*. She hopes to publish at least one book per year. Although she enjoys writing books, Charlay Marie's true passion is to write, produce, and direct inspirational, heartfelt movies. She is currently working on her first film project. Two of her biggest inspirations are Oprah Winfrey and Tyler Perry. Charlay Marie writes, directs, and lives in Columbus, Ohio with plans of moving to New York to continue her career.

UC HIS GLORY BOOK CLUB!

www.uchisglorybookclub.net

UC His Glory Book Club is the spirit-inspired brain-child of Joylynn Ross, Author and Acquisitions Editor of Urban Christian, and Kendra Norman-Bellamy, Author for Urban Christian. This is an online book club that hosts authors of Urban Christian. We welcome as members all men and women who have a passion for reading Christian-based fiction.

UC His Glory Book Club pledges our commitment to provide support, positive feedback, encouragement, and a forum whereby members can openly discuss and review the literary works of Urban Christian authors.

There is no membership fee associated with UC His Glory Book Club; however, we do ask that you support the authors through purchasing, encouraging, providing book reviews, and of course, your prayers. We also ask that you respect our beliefs and follow the guidelines of the book club. We hope to receive your valuable input, opinions, and reviews that build up, rather than tear down our authors.

What We Believe:

—We believe that Jesus is the Christ, Son of the Living God.

—We believe the Bible is the true, living Word of God.

—We believe all Urban Christian authors should use their God-given writing abilities to honor God and share the message of the written word God has given to each of them uniquely.

—We believe in supporting Urban Christian authors in their literary endeavors by reading, purchasing and sharing their titles with our online community.

—We believe that in everything we do in our literary arena should be done in a manner that will lead to God being glorified and honored.

We look forward to the online fellowship with you.

Please visit us often at *www.uchisglorybookclub.net*.

Many Blessing to You!

Shelia E. Lipsey,
President, UC His Glory Book Club